The Hitman's

Pregnant

Bride

I0562490

Alyse Zaftig

ISBN: 978-1634810548

Breakfast in Bed

Andreas

Andreas made a lot of noise on each step so Phoebe could hear him coming up the stairs. He liked to spoil his wife. He walked slowly enough for her to wake up. The tray was heavy, a sturdy wood that could handle two heavy plates of food and two mugs. One had coffee for Andreas; the other had hot chocolate for Phoebe, since the doctor had told them that she needed to stay away from caffeine while she was trying to get pregnant.

Andreas and Phoebe had been trying to have a baby for a few

months now. They hadn't used any contraception at all, and Andreas knew that Phoebe was getting a little stressed out about not being pregnant yet. He didn't mind all the practice, though; Andreas knew that the time would come. They just had to be patient.

Phoebe had been very quiet for a few days, so Andreas decided that today would be a bacon kind of day.

"Good morning, darling."

"Good morning," Phoebe said. She beamed at him. "Is that bacon I smell?"

"Yep." Andreas put the tray down on the nightstand. "I don't work for free, you know. Pay up." He leaned in close to his wife. Phoebe got on her knees so that she could kiss him, twining their tongues together in the way that Phoebe knew that he liked. She was the best wife in the whole world.

Picking up a fork, Andreas carefully fed the rest of her breakfast to her, cutting her pancakes, scooping up her scrambled eggs, and hand-feeding her the rest of the bacon. He didn't care about his breakfast.

When her plate was clean, Andreas grinned at her before diving in for another kiss. Andreas tugged at the strings of her bathrobe, revealing acres of smooth, dark skin. He kissed the slopes of her breasts, then he made his way down the center of her body to find her core. The tray of food was forgotten as her hands settled in his hair, guiding his head where she wanted it to be.

He licked her delicate lower lips carefully, humming in pleasure at the sweet taste. Her smell was unique, and he totally loved going down on her. It was his favorite activity in the bedroom, bar none.

He spread her thighs a little bit further apart as he delved more deeply into her body. His nose stimulated her clitoris while his tongue searched the soft lips of her slit. She was shuddering beneath him, crying out, trying to move her hips, but his hands kept her in place. She screamed as her body contracted again and again.

Before she had stopped, Andreas was pushing himself into her, a hand on her clitoris to keep her orgasm going on and on. She was panting, gasping for breath, and Andreas slammed into his wife again and again, plunging into her as deeply as he could, trying to plant the seed that would grow into their baby.

Head going side to side, her hands gripped the sheets and she cried out as she went over the edge a second time. Andreas grunted when he felt her body squeezing his. Then he released inside of her, collapsing on her body with the intensity of his orgasm. He felt as if the top of his head would blow off.

When he could think again, he rolled to the side so that he didn't crush Phoebe.

"Good morning, darling," he told her. She wiggled so that her head rested on his chest.

"Good morning," Phoebe said, her arm going around his body. "You can give me breakfast in bed anytime."

"I will." He pulled one of her hands into his and kissed the back of it. "You know I will."

George Hebus

Andreas

"Baby, as much as I wish I could stay here with you, I've got to go to work."

Phoebe yawned. "That's okay. I'll just lie here."

Andreas bent down and hit her shoulder, making her tilt her head back, her dark hair all over the pillow.

"I love you."

"Always," Phoebe told him.

Andreas quickly showered and pulled on some clothes before blowing a kiss to his sleepy wife and heading downstairs to drive to work.

When he go to Chung's, there was a nondescript beige delivery truck idling outside. When he got out of his car, the driver, who was wearing a blue uniform without any kind of insignia, walked up to him.

"Andreas?"

"That's me." Andreas adjusted his stance. He couldn't draw a gun fast enough to take this guy, but if he needed to, he'd momentarily incapacitate him so he could get his gun out of his ankle holster.

"Package. I'll need you to sign for it."

Andreas took the offered pen and wrote his symbol there. In the criminal underworld, nobody used his actual signature; everybody knew him simply as A.

"Thank you," he told the delivery man.

The delivery man nodded at him before getting back into his car and driving off.

Andreas tucked it under his arm and went inside of the back door of the restaurant. Getting out a knife, Andreas opened the package that had just arrived when he got inside of Chung's kitchen. When he heard chimes, his eyes flicked up to check that Mei Lung was still talking to the wealthy customer who always asked about trying blowfish. No matter what Mei told him, he never opted to get it. He always got something safer in the end. Andreas smiled to himself. That guy had made a serious ritual out of inquiring about blowfish and never actually getting the nerve to try it. He put on an apron just to keep up with appearances; it would be weird to have a guy dressed in normal clothes in the kitchen of a busy restaurant like Chung's.

Pulling a small envelope out of a bag of flour in the delivery box, Andreas looked around the whole kitchen to make sure that he was alone. Biting his bottom lip, he carefully opened the envelope.

Inside of the envelope, there was a small card with a name at the top of it: George Hebus. The card also listed the kills and crimes against humanity that had brought the man to the Agency's attention. He was a dead man walking now.

Tucking the card into his back pocket, Andreas removed the bags of flour from the box and put them in the right spot in the pantry. Grabbing the vial tucked into a satchel at the bottom of the box, he tucked it in the same pocket as the card, removed his apron, and headed out to run some initial surveillance on his next target.

Initial Surveillance

Andreas

Andreas checked his watch, knowing George should be walking out in the next minute. Right on time, George walked out of the restaurant. Andreas knew that it was time. The setting fit the request, and his employers always liked for symbolism to strike at the heart of their enemies.

Andreas punched in seven digits, the seven digits that made up George's office number.

Ring.

"Hello! Marley speaking. How can I help you?"

"Hello, Marley. My name is Drake. I would like to set up a meeting with George. I'd like to talk to him over a dinner meeting." Andreas had another identity as Drake Vanderhoff, a nondescript businessman who had enough documents to back him up.

"I see, Mr. Drake. Could I ask what you'd like to talk to him about?"

"It's a matter requiring some discretion."

"I see." The receptionist paused.

Andreas' eyes went to the picture of his beautiful wife dangling from his rearview mirror. He had to tear his eyes away. His line of work wasn't sustainable at all, but he couldn't think about Phoebe at the moment.

Soon they'd have a baby on the way, and Andreas needed to do more jobs to pull together the capital which would mean that he could settle into a quiet, idyllic life where his major concern was raising their kid. Just a few more jobs before he could retire from the business, going dark. He'd become an actual chef and focus on his catering front so he could turn it into a real business. The infrastructure already existed. He'd done enough for the moment. He drove towards his house.

When he finally got home, Andreas counted his breaths as he slowly breathed in and out. Outside of the house, he always shed his work persona like a snake shed skin.

The artichoke rangoons that he whipped up in Chung's kitchen were in a bag on the floor on the passenger's seat. The smell of the oil filled his car. He always brought something home for Phoebe; it was necessary to maintain his front.

When he was as calm as he was going to get, he walked out of his car and up the steps into his kitchen.

"Hey, baby."

Phoebe was wearing an apron and pulling a cookie sheet out of the oven. He admired the curve of her hips.

"Oh, Andreas! You're a little early. I wanted the cookies to cool down before you came home. I tried something new — I added double the amount of peanut butter and put in a little pudding mix."

"Pudding mix?" Andreas was a better cook, but Phoebe was a phenomenal baker.

"For texture. One of my friends told me about it — she swore that she wouldn't make cookies without pudding ever again."

Andreas shrugged. Phoebe put the cookie sheet down on a rack to cool. As soon as it was out of her hands, Andreas quickly prowled across the kitchen to draw his sweet-smelling wife into his arms and lean her back for a hard kiss.

He finally put her back on her own feet. "Good evening, Phoebe."

"Hi," she said, her arms around

him. "Phew. You kiss me like that every day, but I never get used to it."

He kissed her temple. "How was your day, sweetheart?"

"Well, I got a record number of sales today!"

"Really?"

"Yeah! Double my best day so far. I have so much work to do! I barely regret giving up the troupe for a little while."

Andreas and Phoebe had talked about her performance schedule. If she was going to have their baby, she needed to take some maternity leave for a season, maybe two, maybe more. Her boss had let her go; there were always more girls who were eager to dance in their troupe.

Phoebe had turned her attention to her doll business, Destiny Dolls. They were soft ballerina dolls that she made with love and sold on Etsy. Dance was Phoebe's core, and she had to tap into it one way or another while she was on hiatus. She would go crazy otherwise.

"That's wonderful, babe."

Andreas went to the wine cabinet, pulling out a small Copa di Vino to grab some merlot and a small plastic bottle of Welch's grape juice.

"We should celebrate."

Even though Phoebe wasn't pregnant yet, it was never too early to start taking some common-sense precautions. Andreas poured his wine into a glass and poured her grape juice into another one. The two glasses were nearly identical.

He turned around and gave her the glass of juice.

"Cheers for your business' success, Phoebe!"

They clinked their glasses and each took a sip before Andreas touched Phoebe's stomach. It looked a little bigger than usual, though he'd never tell her that.

"I have some news," she said, clearing her throat.

"Yeah?"

She took a deep breath before saying, "I'm pregnant."

Andreas immediately put down his glass and pulled Phoebe into the air, spinning her around.

"Andreas! You spilled my juice!" But Phoebe was laughing in his arms, and the rebuke didn't sting.

"I'll clean it up later. Right now, there's something that needs a little more attention."

He didn't have the time to take her upstairs to their bed. He swept Phoebe off of her feet and put her gently on the couch. He stole her wine glass from her and put it on their coffee table.

"Are you wearing underwear?"

"Andreas!"

"Are you?"

"No," she whispered.

Happy

Andreas

He bit her thigh, pushing her dress up to her waist. "Dirty girl." Andreas knew that she'd anticipated his response to her announcement. He was over the moon about their child, and he'd make sure that she knew it in her bones.

The couch limited some positions, but he'd make it work. He knelt on the ground beside the couch and let his five o'clock shadow rub against the juncture of her thighs. She moaned and bucked her hips upwards.

"Patience, darling."

"Mmm."

He bit the inside of one soft, dark-skinned thigh and then the other.

"More," she demanded, jerking her hips upwards.

"Greedy girl," he told her. But he lowered his tongue to her slit anyway.

"Ah," she breathed.

Now Andreas brought one of his hands to rub her clit, circling it again and again until she was going wild beneath him on the couch, wet enough to make a puddle. He'd fix it, just like the juice, later, but right now he'd bask in masculine pride from giving his woman pleasure.

He drank down all of her juice

that he could by meticulously licking every bit of her inner parts, as she shook through one orgasm and then another.

When he was a little concerned about her running out of oxygen, he rested, one cheek against her thigh.

"That was amazing," she panted.

"You're amazing, babe." He lifted his head and met her eyes. "I'm so happy about the baby."

"I'm glad."

Andreas pulled her into a sitting position and then sat down on the couch beside her before pulling her into his lap, her legs straddling his. He bit her ear hard, making her gasp.

"I'm glad that you're taking a break to focus on your business and the baby."

"Me, too."

"Is there anything you'd like now that we have the baby?"

"I want to have dinner with my parents."

Andreas felt like Phoebe had dumped a bucket of ice water over his head as part of the Ice Bucket Challenge. His blood, which had been running hot after eating her on the couch, cooled to subzero temperatures.

He internally sighed, already exhausted by just the mention of Phoebe's FBI agent father.

"Why?"

An uncomfortable silence settled between them for a moment.

"This time, I'll make sure that Daddy is nice. He'll come around and accept you into the family eventually, you know."

"You keep telling me that, sweetheart, but it hasn't happened yet." He put his hands in her hair and pulled her in for a fast kiss, ending the conversation. "Now how about we go upstairs and spend some time in a big, soft bed, hm?"

Phoebe kissed him back in response, which was everything that he needed. He carried his pregnant wife up the stairs in record time before dropping her on the bed and climbing on top of her, biting her neck, pinning her wrists, and making her moan.

And that was just the appetizer.

Fatal Dinner

Andreas

The next evening, Andreas grabbed a piece of bread from the bread basket. He dipped the bread into the little dish of olive oil which had several different herbs and spices floating inside of it.

"Thank you for meeting me for dinner." He'd told Phoebe that he had a business dinner to attend, which was true. She didn't need to know the details or that he would be killing his dinner companion shortly.

Andreas looked like the CEO of a business, which he was. Of course, the outside world believed that he was the CEO of a catering business, even though his true trade dealt in guns and death.

"Thank you for paying for my dinner. I hope that you feel comfortable paying for saltimbocca. It's the most expensive thing on their menu."

"Of course," Andreas said, inclining his head. It figured that George would take all that he could get from this random stranger. It fit with the profile that Andreas had been given by the Agency.

"Do you want wine to go with it?"

"What would you suggest?"

"How about a nice Chardonnay?"

"Sure."

Andreas signaled the sommelier to come over to their table.

"A bottle of Chardonnay, please."

The sommelier nodded and said, "Right away." In a few minutes, he brought the bottle to their table in an ice bucket. Andreas and George watched while the sommelier uncorked the bottle and began to pour a little into their wine glasses. Drinking wine with a target was vastly different from drinking wine with Phoebe.

Andreas shook off the thought of his beautiful, pregnant wife. She didn't belong anywhere near the filth that he got on his hands when he went to work every day.

"What can I get you?" The waiter

finally made it to their table.

"I'll take saltimbocca."

"Ravioli al forno."

"Right away."

"So, what brings you to this restaurant? It certainly isn't to spend hundreds of dollars on wine," George chortled, his face turning red as he laughed and then coughed. Andreas held back a sigh. If he didn't poison George, George would probably kill himself just from leading a life of excess.

"I'll get to business in a minute, but what if we just hang on for a moment? I have to visit the facilities."

"Of course. I'll just help myself to a little more of your wine."

"Please do. Just a moment."

Andreas went to the restaurant's bathrooms, which were handily close to the kitchen. He shed his jacket. In one of his pockets, he had a crumpled apron. He walked into the restaurant's busiest area.

The key to being discreet was looking as if he actually belonged there, which he did. On one level, he was a chef. He'd practically grown up in the kitchen with a mother who had no time to look after him. He mostly tried to stay out of trouble while she worked. On a second level, this was his job. He definitely had to keep on going for as long as he could, so that he could afford to take care of his family.

He had a vial of Death Camas

inside of his pocket as he spied the saltimbocca that George had ordered. He hoped that George really enjoyed it, because it would be the last meal that George ever ate. There were many people working, but none of them were looking at him. Andreas knew how to disappear in a crowd. He quickly emptied the contents of the vial — odorless, colorless, basically undetectable because it looked like salt — onto the saltimbocca before concealing the empty vial in his pocket again and nonchalantly leaving.

To maintain his cover, he walked into the bathroom, used the facilities, washed his dirty hands, and dried them before going back to the table just in time to see their waiter bring their food.

"Perfect timing," George told Andreas.

"Do you need anything else?" the waiter asked.

"No, we're good," George told him.

"I love saltimbocca, but my wife never lets me have it. Too much cholesterol." Small talk, yeah, but it hit Andreas in the chest. He thought about Phoebe, thought about someone else saying the same thing to him. Was he in the right line of work if his conscience was going to pinch him like this?

"Excuse me...I have to take a call." Andreas picked up his phone and made his way outside, his ravioli al forno still untouched on the table.

George was still enthusiastically eating the poison that would kill him quickly. It didn't leave many traces, but whatever was left would be carefully processed and concealed by the Agency, which had long ago penetrated the law enforcement of most urban centers. A policeman would catalogue the food and the coroner would do an autopsy that showed the last traces of the poison inside of George's corpse, but all of that would be doctored and washed away by the Agency's employees. They always got what they wanted. Andreas may have been the one to put Death Camas in the food, but he was under their spell. If he hadn't done it, one of the other people from the Agency would've brought death to George Hebus, no matter what Andreas chose.

He was outside when he turned around just in time to watch George fall head-first onto his plate of saltimbocca.

Andreas walked away quickly enough to disappear but slowly enough not to arouse any suspicion. When he was four blocks away, he pulled out his phone, typing in *555 to log the completed job.

He caught the eye of a homeless man who had a styrofoam cup for change. Andreas pulled a $20 bill out of his pocket, depositing it in the cup. The man touched his nose, and

Andreas knew that the homeless man would forget him quickly, spending the money and watching it disappear.

"What's my emergency? There's a problem with my heart. I keep feeling..." Andreas kept up a fast patter while he walked away from the street corner and the homeless man whose suspicions had been aroused. He turned a corner and quickly disappeared from sight.

He was sloppy to be noticed by anyone at all. He thought that the homeless man was far enough away from the restaurant for police to miss him in their investigation of the area; the Agency could fix things if he was noticed, but it was better not to leave any traces at all.

Gas Station and Chung's

Andreas

Andreas saw a gas station and headed straight inside for the bathroom, which was in a narrow hallway in the back. He barely made it into a stall to lose his lunch in the toilet, wiped his mouth with toilet paper, and then he went to the sink to wash his dirty hands.

He looked into his own eyes. The time when he could do a kill and walk away unscathed was gone. Empathy was the mind-killer here. That comment that George had made about his wife messed with Andreas' head. Yeah, she could be as evil, as cruel, as George, but what if she was a beautiful housewife like Phoebe who greeted her husband at night with a kiss and some freshly baked cookies? He imagined Phoebe baking cookies one night and getting a call that her husband, the father of her child, would never come home again. Andreas dry heaved into the sink with that thought. He definitely needed to make sure that, even if he died on one of his last jobs, Phoebe would be well taken care of.

He got out of the bathroom and walked to the door. It was raining outside and there was a neon orange sign that proclaimed that a cheap umbrella cost two dollars. He paid in cash, picking change out of his back pocket for the tax.

"Thank you. Have a great day," the bored teenager with out of control acne behind the counter told him. Andreas could tell that the teenager wished that his shift was over.

"You too."

Andreas opened the umbrella outside, walking slowly to his car, which was parked two blocks south. It was windy, and Andreas fought to keep his umbrella up when faced with the force of the wind. When he got to his car, he closed the umbrella and shook it out before coming inside. He tossed it on the passenger side's floor and opened the glove compartment, where he kept his wedding ring inside of the owner's manual. He slipped it back on his finger, the ring sliding easily on the moisture from the rain that had hit him when the wind picked up.

He started the car and drove back to Chung's, where he could take a shower and wash himself of the sin that he had committed tonight. He snuck in the back and turned on the small shower in the back room. He grabbed a towel off of the rack. Chung made sure that there were always clean towels stocked for anybody who came through. Chung got a regularly monthly payment to avoid any questions and sometimes handle a little clean up or paperwork. He was still toweling off his hair when he came out of the bathroom.

"Beer?" Sitting in the corner, Chung raised his own bottle. He had another bottle in his other hand, an unopened one.

Andreas tossed the towel over his shoulder and took the beer, which had a twist-off cap.

"Rough night."

"Maybe."

"Take a load off. Chill for a minute."

"I can't. I'm going to whip up something for Phoebe and head home. She just thought that I was working the late dinner shift."

"Already done." Chung showed him a white box.

Andreas felt a shiver go down his

spine. It was chilling just how well the Agency knew about his life. Andreas opened the box to find a square of tiramisu that terrified Andreas completely, making his hands shake when the murder hadn't made them shake for a second. He knew that Chung's restaurant didn't sell tiramisu; the only reason why it had been made was solely for Phoebe. Andreas would throw it away; it could be laced with poison. He might be overly paranoid because he'd just poisoned George's food, but he couldn't tell Chung that he was suspicious. He'd trust him with Agency work, but he didn't know if he would trust him with everything.

"Thank you very much."

Andreas nodded at Chung. "I should go home."

"Say hello to your wife."

Andreas didn't want to think about Chung knowing too much about his family, so he just left. He quickly threw the bag into the dumpster on the way out.

As he started his car, his mind was racing. He used to be able to handle the work and force the kills to the back of his mind, but ever since he married Phoebe, it wasn't easy to chase them away. He wanted to be a better man for her sake. He had pretended to be a normal chef because that's what she expected from him. Though she didn't know it, he had failed her repeatedly.

Even if he wanted to go, he had a contract to fulfill for a few more hits. The contract was to ensure that the Agency was fully reimbursed for his living expenses and training in a number of arts, including culinary school. He had two more jobs left before he fulfilled the terms of the contract.

Dinner with the Kaines

Phoebe

"Sweetheart, we're almost late for dinner."

"Coming," Phoebe called, slipping a bracelet on her wrist. "Just a minute!"

She carefully smoothed down her hair and checked the back view. She had gone shopping with her mother to get this dress a few months ago, and she wanted to make sure that her mother knew that she was using it. Phoebe's mother was very generous when it came to clothing, as long as Phoebe actually used what she bought.

Phoebe ran down the stairs, probably undoing the work that she'd just done. Andreas was standing next to the doorway.

"You look beautiful, babe." He leaned in to kiss her. She kissed him lightly, not wanting to mess up her lip gloss before her parents saw it, although she supposed that eating would mess it up anyway.

"We should go," Phoebe said, wiping her hands on the skirt of the dress. She might have been sweating a little bit, but that was because of her dad and his strange antagonistic attitude towards Andreas.

The car ride was quiet, the radio filling the silence. When they got to her parents' home, the one where she'd grown up, she was out the door and walking up the steps while Andreas turned off the car and trailed behind her. The air was filled with the scent of cinnamon, and she knew that her mom had baked pumpkin pie, which was Andreas' favorite.

"Hello, munchkin."

"Daddy!" Phoebe went and hugged her father. "I'm so happy to see you. Where's Mommy?"

"Here, kiddo." Her mother smelled like vanilla and cinnamon; she definitely had been baking. "And where's Andreas?"

"Here, ma'am." Phoebe had tried to break him of the habit of calling her parents ma'am and sir, but

Andreas still didn't stop. Her mom had tried to convince him to call them Sally and Harold, but it just didn't stick.

"Everything's already on the dinner table."

The four of them went inside of the house, and Phoebe sighed with contentment when she saw the table practically groaning from the weight of the food. Her mother equated food with love, and it was a constant battle to keep her dancer's figure when her mother's delicious and buttery cooking was around.

They sat down at the table and had barely put napkins on their laps when her father said, "You're still a chef, right?"

"That's right."

"So when are you going to get a real job?"

Phoebe watched Andreas wince just a little bit. She put her hand on his. Her father had just hurled one of the standard insults at Andreas, and she could see the tension in Andreas' shoulders. Phoebe hated the way that her father loved to verbally spar with Andreas. He was wonderful, just wonderful, a dream husband and a good man. Why couldn't her father see that?

Yes, the wedding had been a surprise to her close-knit family, but her mother had no problem baking pumpkin pies (Andreas' favorite) and bringing them over for Phoebe and

Andreas to share. She knew that her father had been upset that there'd been basically nobody from Andreas' side at the wedding, but it wasn't as if he could control the fact that he was an orphan. Being an orphan didn't make him a bad man.

In fact, her father should be trying even harder to embrace him and show him how warm their family could be.

"I have a real job, sir," Andreas said, wiping his mouth.

"And no family, is that right?"

Phoebe's mouth tightened, her eyes filling with tears. Her pregnancy was making her really emotional.

And nauseous.

"Excuse me."

She ran out the door and towards the bathroom.

Leftovers

Andreas

Andreas looked at Mr. Kaine, wiping his mouth again.

"Thank you for the wonderful dinner, Mr. and Mrs. Kaine. I'll need to call it a night. We'll leave once Phoebe is done in the bathroom. I don't want Phoebe or the new baby dealing with too much stress, but I highly enjoyed this delicious meal."

Mr. Kaine just grunted, but Mrs. Kaine rose to her feet and tucked a dark strand of hair behind her ear.

"Why don't I pack up some leftovers for you two? I know that you're a chef, but surely you could do with a little more."

"No, it won't be necessary. Thank you for the offer."

"I insist." Mrs. Kaine bustled toward the kitchen. Andreas didn't sigh. Mrs. Kaine meant well.

Andreas looked at Mr. Kaine again and left the room, waiting next to the door of the bathroom to wait for Phoebe to come out. He didn't want the extra food from Mrs. Kaine, but he couldn't politely decline the offer once she pushed it on him.

The door to the bathroom opened and his wife came out. He put an arm around her shoulders.

"You okay?"

"Yeah," she sniffled, "but I want

to go home. I really don't feel very good."

He leaned down and kissed her temple. "We can make that happen."

"I have your food!" Mrs. Kaine announced as she stepped into the hallway. Andreas could see that it was in a pretty green bag, one of the ones that Mrs. Kaine used for shopping at the farmer's market. He internally groaned; it was a really nice bag, one that they'd have to return sooner rather than later, which meant that he had to sit through Mr. Kaine's interrogation sometime soon.

Joy.

Phoebe was still crying softly as they waved goodbye to her parents, but all of them pretended that it wasn't happening.

Phoebe and Andreas got into the car and buckled up. As Andreas put the car in reverse, Phoebe opened the glove compartment and used the brown fast food napkins to blow her nose. She wadded them up in her hand.

The drive was quiet until Andreas decided to break the silence.

"How are you feeling?"

"Okay," Phoebe said, even though she was still clearly crying. She turned away from him and looked out the window, her fist clenching around the wadded up napkins.

Ugly Cry

Phoebe

Phoebe looked out the window because she knew that she was an ugly crier. She knew that she was married to Andreas, but that didn't mean that she wanted him to see her with a blotchy nose and red eyes. She looked like a hideous monster when she cried. These pregnancy hormones were really messing with her system.

Andreas must have turned on the radio, because her favorite song came on. Phoebe smiled for the first time since the dinner with her parents and sang along softly after she turned the volume up.

She realized then that Andreas hadn't turned on the radio. He'd started one of the CDs that he had in his car. He wanted to cheer her up.

She felt way more weepy than she normally was. Phoebe had her ups and downs, true, but she normally kept all of it inside. She didn't cry quite this much.

"Honey, do you want some comfort food? Thin Mint ice cream? We can pick it up on the way home."

Phoebe sniffed again. "I'd like to go to Chung's. Why don't you make me something nice?"

"It's..." Andreas paused. "It's poker night and Chung's had to close early."

Phoebe raised a brow.

"But we can get ice cream."

"No. I'd rather go home so I can sleep."

"We can do that." Phoebe wasn't sure if she could hear relief in Andreas' voice.

They drove for a little longer, then Andreas was turning on the little street that led to their home.

There was a large brown envelope at their front door.

"Andreas, why is there a package at our front door? I haven't ordered anything." Phoebe was an Amazon Prime member, and she was a little bit addicted to ordering packages...but she hadn't ordered any this week.

"I'm not sure." Andreas parked the car in the garage, which automatically opened when it sensed that his car was near it. "Let me check, okay, babe? Why don't you head upstairs. I'll make some tea and be right up."

"Okay."

Phoebe went up the stairs and yawned as she got to the top step. She covered her mouth with her hand. She was wiped out, even though they hadn't stayed at her parents' house very long for dinner.

She went to the bathroom to take off her makeup and get into her jammies. Her favorite pajamas were soft blue pajamas with pictures of sheep on them, and Andreas had told her that they were adorable.

Her eyelids felt like they weighed a hundred pounds, so she got into her bed and rested her eyes for just a few minutes while she waited for Andreas to come upstairs with her tea.

Waking Up

Phoebe

Phoebe woke up the next morning. She must have fallen asleep before Andreas came upstairs. He was beside her, his morning wood evident beneath the sheet. As soon as she noticed it, she knew how she wanted to say good morning.

She threw the covers off and parted his legs. He normally slept naked, which was definitely a plus. She lowered her head at the right angle to take his erection into her mouth. He woke up as soon as she touched her mouth to the top of his cock.

"Oh," he moaned. "Yes."

Phoebe stroked the shaft with her hand, pumping him up. She used her other hand to fondle his balls.

"Ah," Andreas said as he released his seed into her mouth. He pumped several shots inside of her.

"Good morning, Phoebe."

"Morning, husband."

Phoebe took off her pajamas quickly. Andreas could easily go two rounds.

"Sit up."

Andreas quickly sat up in the bed, and Phoebe put her thighs on the outside of his thighs. She kissed his mouth. His hands went to her hips, guiding her even closer to him than she already was.

"Ready?"

She bit her lip and nodded. He eased her down on his still-hard erection.

Phoebe had been married to Andreas for a little while now, but she still wasn't used to just how big he was. He stretched her to her limits, just to the edge between pain and pleasure. Her eyes were shut as he finally pushed all the way inside of her.

Then she opened her eyes and braced her arms around his neck as she began to move. Up. Down. She rocked on top of him, her pace increasing as she got closer to her own completion.

Then Andreas bit her neck, which made her skyrocket. She saw stars behind her closed eyelids, her body flushing with white heat. She could feel him releasing for a second time inside of her, filling her with warmth.

Their lovemaking was always intense; she had to admit that morning sex was one of her favorite things to do, and Andreas frequently indulged in her taste for it.

"I can't believe how lucky I am to be married to you, baby."

"Same goes," Phoebe said, still out of breath from their vigorous morning sex.

"It's okay if your hormones are out of control while you are pregnant. I'll make as many midnight runs to the grocery store as I need to make. If you start going crazy and cleaning everything, that's okay. I love all of you. I'm more in love with you than I ever thought that I could be with a woman."

Phoebe's eyes filled with tears. It could just be pillow talk, but Andreas definitely knew how to start the morning right.

"I love you, too. And I apologize in advance for how crazy I'm going to be during this pregnancy."

"It's just fine, especially if you like waking me up with your mouth." He kissed her softly.

She kissed him back. "I know that last night was a disaster, but my father will come around eventually.

Working for the FBI, he's naturally suspicious of just about everybody. He wants to protect me, but he needs to learn that I'm not his little girl anymore. I can make my own choices, and I choose you."

"I know that your dad is overprotective." He bit his lip.

"What's wrong?" Phoebe said instantly.

"Everything is fine...just fine. Maybe I just need a little more sleep."

Phoebe knew that he was closing himself off from her, but she smiled anyway. "Let's both go back to sleep." Her cheek was resting against his chest. She still felt a little bit of her post-orgasm warm glow inside, and her breathing slowed until she finally fell back asleep.

Chip's Coffee

Andreas

Andreas waited until Phoebe's breathing changed to get out of bed. He went to use the downstairs shower to clean up after their phenomenal morning sex. He had made a pot of chamomile tea for Phoebe last night, but it had really been an excuse to stay downstairs for long enough to hide the package behind one of their bookshelves.

He was still naked when he opened up the envelope with a small knife that he kept in his desk drawer. The only things that the Agency would send to the house would be learning materials for major operations that were too sensitive to send electronically. It was something that he didn't really want to think about when he had a baby on the way. He couldn't imagine that he was the only agent who was qualified for the job.

Clenching his jaw, he walked back upstairs so that he could get dressed. Phoebe was still asleep as he got ready to head into work.

He left a note that said "I love you" for Phoebe, since he wouldn't wake her up before he went to work.

Then he drove to Chip's coffee shop, the worst coffee shop in the city with the foulest, most bitter variation of coffee. The only reason he was there was because he needed to talk to his handler. Chip's was where they could make contact discreetly, although if anybody trailed Andreas, they would recognize that either he was addicted to extremely foul coffee or he worked for the Agency. Having a standard home base was a risk, but everything in life was a risk. It was easier to stay in touch when he knew where to go.

He only had to pretend to drink the bitter coffee for a few minutes before his handler came out.

"Monsieur X," Andreas said, getting to his feet to shake his handler's hand. "What a pleasure."

"The pleasure is mine, I'm sure."

Part French, part Vietnamese, Monsieur X didn't have any other names. Privately, Andreas wondered if his name might be Xavier or something, but he wasn't audacious enough to ask.

"Why did you come in for a meeting, Andreas?"

"I wanted to ask for a reassignment."

"Oh?"

"I saw the assignment that was sent to my house after the Hebus one. You know that I am capable of it, but somehow my heart isn't in the work anymore."

"There's not a lot that I can do about your assignment, Andreas. If you burn the job, you will endanger your contract. I understand your circumstances, but the Agency feels that you are the best man for the job."

Andreas clenched his jaw and drank another sip of the foul coffee. He set his cup back down before meeting Monsieur X's eyes.

"Is there any way that I can get out of this?"

Sighing, Monsieur X sat back and folded his hands in front of him.

Cleaning and Dinner

Phoebe

Phoebe had a pail full of all of her cleaning supplies. She needed to clean the house from top to bottom. She wasn't fastidious — definitely much more of a slob than her meticulous husband — but she had the urge to clean. When she did clean, she always did a thorough job. She had always been the kind of girl who liked to stay busy. Her mother had told her that idle hands were tools for the devil. Phoebe wasn't quite as religious as her mother, but she realized that she had a powerful need to clean everything. Her mother had warned her, when Phoebe had told her about the baby, that she might have some nesting instincts. Now Phoebe thought that they might be kicking in.

She had been dating Andreas for only a little while when she knew that she was ready to be his wife. He was everything that she could possibly want. Strong, protective, gorgeous, panty-meltingly talented in the kitchen...and she could sense something deep inside of Andreas, something that made her want to heal him. She knew that his childhood as an orphan hadn't been easy. He told her some details from that time in his life, but he kept it under wraps for the most part. It was tucked behind his strong front, but she could sense the neglected soul inside of him. It was part of why she loved him so much. She knew that he felt better when she was around.

She was on her floor, scrubbing the tile of the kitchen, when she realized that she could smell the cleaning fumes. Would they hurt the baby? It was a little late to think of all that today, but she would have to ask her doctor if she should switch to all-natural cleaning supplies. She finished up the kitchen before making her way to the laundry.

They always threw their dirty clothes there and she began to empty the pockets of all of the clothing that had been tossed about. Andreas preferred to do his own laundry, but she could do it today. He seemed so preoccupied lately, and she wasn't sure if that was due to the baby or not.

Inside of his jacket pocket, the one that she would need to put in with a dry-cleaning pack, she could see something the size of a training card with a picture of a man who didn't look anything like an athlete. He looked like the CEO of an IT firm. She raised her eyebrows and set it aside. She had a stack of her own dirty aprons to wash before she made dinner for their Game of Thrones anniversary. They'd clicked from the very start, but their love of Game of

Thrones, which they had both read before HBO had picked up the series, was something that bonded them together. One of the rooms in their house had a huge tapestry of the family trees of all of the characters. The tapestry was very convoluted.

When everything was in the washer, she went to the kitchen and washed her hands before turning on some music. She had been reluctant to download Amazon Music on her phone, but she had to admit that the selection was surprisingly good. She kept her iPhone on a dock with some nice speakers in her kitchen, and sang quietly along with the music as she baked a nice chicken pot pie for Andreas. She stirred all the ingredients together in a pot and par-baked the crust before putting everything together. Her mother had taught her a way to cheat on the top part of the chicken pot pie, using frozen biscuits instead of a pie crust for the top layer, just to make sure that everything was properly cooked through.

When the timer dinged, she took out her silly sheep oven mitts and took the pie out of the oven. She looked at the oven clock. The pie would need to cool for a little while, but it should be ready just in time for Andreas to come home.

The washer chimed, announcing that it was done. She transferred everything she could into the dryer while she hung everything else up to air out or dry out.

Because she didn't want any of the chemicals in their food, Phoebe washed her hands again. She put the chicken pot pie, something that Andreas told her was his favorite, onto a little holder on the dinner table. She set two places with real cloth napkins, which were a wedding present from her mother. They were hand-made and had little ducks on them. She lit two candles and waited.

* * *

Two hours later, the candles were significantly lower. There were two puddles of melted wax at the bottom of the candleholders. She stared at Andreas' spot as if it would make him magically appear. He was very late.

She wouldn't cry. She blew out the candles before she picked up the pot pie, covered it, and put it into the fridge. She looked at the time on the oven. He was hardly ever late.

Phoebe took a quick shower to get the scent of chicken off of her. A couple tears fell in the shower, where there wasn't anybody to see her cry. She dried off and then dressed into her jammies before walking back downstairs so that she could see Andreas when he finally came home. She curled up with a soft Kashwere blanket on their couch and closed her eyes.

Humble Pie

Andreas

As he got into the driveway, Andreas looked at the clock and groaned. He didn't wait for the garage door to fully close before he went inside. He could see that the table was still set with the duck cloth napkins. There wasn't any food.

Damn.

He narrowly stopped himself from sending his fist crashing through the wall. He promised himself, back when he started to get serious about Phoebe, that he wouldn't let the job interfere with his relationship. Now it

---

had. It was bad enough that he was married to an FBI agent's daughter, but now everything was at risk. The Agency had assigned him a job that would definitely raise some red flags for anybody who was looking. He was supposed to do a hit on an FBI agent. Mr. Harold Kaine definitely would find out. Andreas knew that her father would look into everything that happened; it was going to be a gigantic pain in the ass to keep the old man off of his trail.

Sighing, he opened up the fridge to see what Phoebe had cooked for dinner. He remembered that he was supposed to bring her something, but had forgotten it while he had done surveillance for his next target, the conversation that he had with Monsieur X playing in the back of his mind the whole time. He got out the special chicken pot pie, which was a little fancier than Phoebe normally went for a normal dinner.

That was right. Today was their Game of Thrones anniversary. Andreas felt like a terrible husband, both for forgetting about it and for coming home late without remembering to tell Phoebe. He cut a serving of the chicken pot pie and threw it in the oven to broil for just a minute, watching the oven closely before he pulled out the pot pie with some oven mitts.

Sitting down at the kitchen table with the duck napkin in his lap, he ate bite after bite of the absolutely delicious chicken pot pie. When he was done, he cleared his plate and put it into the sink.

A small sigh put him on alert. He walked over towards the TV room. Phoebe was asleep on the couch. He wondered why he hadn't noticed her when he came inside. He had been too wrapped up in his own thoughts, probably.

He pulled her into his arms and carried her upstairs so that they could both go to bed. He put her into bed and tucked her in before going to their bathroom.

Andreas brushed his teeth, undressed, and climbed into bed with his small wife, putting one arm around her. He loved the scent of her shampoo.

He would try to be a better man tomorrow. He'd figure out a way to apologize.

* * *

When Andreas woke up, there was a message waiting on his phone. It only said "Chip's". He knew that he was being called in.

Phoebe was asleep when he went into the bathroom and got ready for the day, getting dressed in their closet before leaving. He dropped a soft kiss on her forehead before he went out the door. She shifted a little bit in her sleep. It was lucky that she was taking some time off for the baby. It helped her sleep a little more than usual.

He walked into Chip's and got his usual, a simple Americano. The coffee was as foul as ever, but it came with an envelope that the barista rested against the coffee mug.

"Thanks," he told the barista, who often changed. They were men and women whose faces were unrecognizable, who could melt into a crowd without any warning.

When he got to an unoccupied table, he opened the envelope. He still hadn't found a way out of this assignment, but he needed to figure something out. He couldn't drop the ball until he found an escape route, though. Phoebe might have faked being asleep this morning before he left for "work," and he had a bad feeling about it. He wondered if he was at risk of driving her away if he came home too late too often.

He drank another sip of the watered down terrible coffee that he always got before opening the envelope.

And sprayed coffee everywhere when he saw the picture of the target.

His target was Harold Kaine, Phoebe's father.

He needed to get out of here. He quickly found a napkin to wipe up the mess and tossed the mostly full cup into the trash.

Then he went into his car but didn't start it. He wasn't in any kind of condition to drive at the moment.

What on earth could he do? His hands gripped the steering wheel hard. Harold Kaine had definitely stepped on the wrong toes. He had been skulking around the Agency, finding the shape of it. Harold Kaine, unlike a lot of their targets, didn't get a death sentence for what he had done. He was getting a death sentence for what he might do: bring down the Agency. It was possible that he had gathered evidence against them. The Agency might want things that he had gathered and not yet turned into the bureau.

Andreas knew that the Agency knew that Harold Kaine was his father-in-law. Was that why Monsieur X had told him that he was the best choice? Did they want him to tie up loose ends? It wasn't a secret that Harold had never liked Andreas, but Andreas had never fantasized about killing Phoebe's dad. It was a nightmare. Andreas was all for working without letting emotions get involved, but this was absolutely ridiculous. He had no intention of killing his father-in-law. It was entirely too far. He hoped that the job wasn't what it looked like.

Starting the Job

Andreas

The next day, Andreas knew that the job was in fact exactly what it looked like. He was running recon on Phoebe's father's habits. It was easier to think about and to speculate about than actually do. Harold Kaine was very cautious with his movements. He was investigating the Agency off the books, which only made him more careful. If Andreas wasn't on the other side, he would be impressed by Harold Kaine's mindfulness. He wasn't an old FBI agent by luck alone. The stupid ones died.

Harold stopped at a food truck parked near one of the secret FBI buildings in DC for lunch. When he heard a motorcycle approach his parked van, Andreas took his eyes off of Harold for just a half second.

But that was long enough for Harold to disappear into the sea of people on the street at lunchtime.

Andreas was done for the day. It was better to hang back than try to get out of the van and find Harold in the sea of people. He had enough problems with Phoebe's father as it was. Looking at his watch, Andreas said, "Damn." He told Phoebe that he'd be home for lunch, skipping the lunch shift and bringing her food.

Andreas started up the van so

that he could head back to Chung's as fast as he could go. There he pulled together some beef noodle soup, a recipe that he'd learned from a Taiwanese street vendor on a mission a long time ago, before he went home to her, the soup carefully put into a bag.

With the soup in his car, he drove home to his wife.

"Phoebe," he called as he entered the house, the bag in hand. "I brought you some lunch."

"It's past two."

"Sorry, babe. I had to pinch-hit for one of our line cooks who didn't show up."

"You could've called."

"It was a last minute thing. I'm

really sorry." Andreas would have to figure out a way to show up on time for his wife. Could Siri remind him to consistently come home on time? He'd have to look into it.

"What did you bring?"

"Beef noodle soup."

"The kind with ketchup?" Her eyes lit up.

"Yup." He started unpacking the bag and putting the contents on their dining room table. "Do you want to get some soup spoons out?" They had big soup spoons that were perfect for this dish. Andreas worked at a Chinese restaurant — or pretended to work at a Chinese restaurant, anyway — so they kept chopsticks on hand.

When the table was set, Phoebe sat down across from him and took a spoonful of the soup.

"Wow, this is so good!"

"Thanks, babe." Andreas took a small sip. It was a little cooler than he'd like, but he had literally thrown it together as fast as he possibly could. He had to keep better track of things; he had a primal need to take care of his wife. There were thin slices of beef brisket on the top, which he had cooked in the hot soup. The slices were a little raw, but Phoebe didn't say anything about it.

"I made a beautiful doll today."

"Yeah?" Andreas ate another bite.

"It's the best one I've ever made yet. I'm so happy about it."

"That's wonderful, babe."

She dropped her chopsticks.

"I know that you get really busy at the restaurant, Andreas. It's okay that you were late."

"Thanks, babe."

"I know we've talked about you taking time to test dishes, deliver on your commitments, and attend all those culinary conventions that pull you away overnight, but the most important part to me is that you come home."

"I appreciate it, honey." He squeezed her hand. "Eat your soup before it goes cold."

They ate in silence. Finally, Andreas stared at the empty bowl in front of him.

"That was really good," Phoebe said. He looked over. Her bowl was totally clean.

"Let's throw all this into the trash." Andreas quickly stacked their bowls and tossed their utensils into the sink.

"Do you need to go back to the restaurant?"

"No, I'm off for the dinner shift." Andreas turned back around to look at his wife.

Her shirt was off, and her stomach looked a little softer than usual.

She didn't need to say much. He liked seeing all of her soft, smooth skin. Her curves seemed even curvier than usual.

Andreas pulled his wife into his arms, sealing his mouth to hers. He was glad that the dining room table had been cleared, because he lifted his small wife and put her on top of it. He only broke the kiss so he could remove her bra and jeans along with her underwear. Andreas pulled off his own shirt and pants. Everything was on the floor. When he was totally naked, he knelt in front of her. He pulled her thighs apart so he could give her a deep kiss between her thighs. She moaned in front of him while he ate her. She tasted better than the soup that he made, that was for sure. He touched her clitoris until he felt her muscles contract again and again as she climaxed, then got to his feet and pulled her legs over his shoulders. She was small, it was true, but she also had the flexibility of a dancer, a fact that he loved when they were in the bedroom.

Or out of it, as the case might be.

He pushed just the tip inside of her. Her eyes flew open and met his. Phoebe looked softer than usual, a little more vulnerable than she usually was. It was almost as if she was asking him wordlessly to trust her and let her all the way in, but he could never tell her the truth. She had everything that he could give anyone, but he couldn't tell her what his real job was. If he told her that he was a mercenary, a hitman, she would leave. He knew it in his heart.

His mouth crashed downwards onto hers and she put her tongue in his mouth, flicking it while he took her small body over and over. Finally, she moaned into his mouth as she milked his cock, getting all of his seed as he released inside of her.

"You okay?" she asked when they could both think again.

"Everything is okay. More than okay," he said, pressing inside of her again. He hadn't gone down yet.

She gave him a smile, but he could tell that it was halfhearted. He didn't know what to tell her. "Hey, baby, rough day at the office. I was just told to kill your dad. By the way, I'm a hitman, just FYI. Great news, huh?" He couldn't tell her.

"Let's stay in bed for the rest of the day, okay, baby? I promise that I'll try to be on time for our next lunch date. How about tomorrow?"

She slid off of the table. "Sounds good to me."

Andreas leaned down to kiss her slowly before carrying her upstairs to spend a little time together. Their marriage was so blissful, better than anything that Andreas could have imagined as a kid. He didn't want to screw it up.

Breaking and Entering

Andreas

The next morning, instead of drinking some terrible coffee, Andreas hit some of the bags in the gym that the Agency kept behind Chip's. Andreas alternated his strikes, changing up his combinations. He needed to clear his mind. His next step was to break into Harold Kaine's house, which would normally be a ludicrous idea. Now it was essential. He had a terrible feeling in his gut about it. He'd been to the Kaines' house many times as a guest; now he'd be an intruder in the house where Phoebe grew up.

He sighed. One more job after Harold Kaine, then he could hang up his guns. He could throw them into the Potomac for all the Agency cared. Just one more. He had to figure a way out of killing Harold and some way to get through two more jobs for the safety of Phoebe and their unborn child. He just had to.

He took a lightning quick shower before getting on the road. Mrs. Kaine's Google schedule kept track of everything that she and Harold did, and Andreas had hacked into it. Harold was supposed to go to a chiropractor first thing this morning. He had an old elbow injury that he treated with regular visits there.

Andreas drove to the doctor's office. When he saw that Harold's car was definitely parked outside, he let out a long breath, steeling himself for the task ahead. Mrs. Kaine had a mani-pedi scheduled until noon, and he needed to be out of the house by then. He finally got there, his heart beating in his chest. He wasn't sure what was going to happen. If he was caught breaking into his in-law's home, how would Phoebe react? He felt just a little bit of sweat pop out on the back of his neck.

He picked the front door's lock. When this was over, he'd tell the Kaines to replace the locks. They weren't particularly complex. Andreas headed for Harold's office, where he saw Harold's locked filing cabinet. He quickly picked the lock on the cabinet.

He heard the floor creak overhead. Had he been caught? No, it was impossible. He was a professional. The house was just settling. His mind was playing tricks on him because he was in his father-in-law's house searching through the private files of someone who already hated him. He needed to get a grip.

There was nothing of interest in the filing cabinet, so he turned his attention to the bookshelves behind Mr. Kaine's desk. He pulled out a huge volume of Merriam-Webster's Unabridged Dictionary. He saw a glint of metal behind it.

Bingo.

He pulled out volume after volume until he saw the dial that would open the safe. He got out his listening device from his pocket while he spun the wheel incredibly slowly, waiting for the tumblers to fall. When he opened the safe, he heard another creak overhead. He quickly emptied the safe, putting everything into his satchel, before he replaced all the books just as he'd found them. There wasn't anybody at home, he knew, but he needed to get home to Phoebe anyway. He had promised her that he wouldn't be late to another lunch date.

Poison

Phoebe

Phoebe turned on the TV while she was cleaning out the basement before lunch. Maybe they could turn it into a playroom for the baby. It was unfinished at the moment, but the contractor that they'd had come by to give them a quote had told them a number that didn't seem too unreasonable. Right now, it was half of a man cave. It wasn't really furnished besides a TV and a couch, but it was where Andreas went to have some alone time and watch football games.

She listened with half an ear to the local news channel as she swept the floor.

Something made her turn around and stare at the TV, the broom in her hand. The news report said that a sudden death of a local businessman had been ruled an accidental poisoning. The man was a well-known eager forager and he had brewed the wrong leaves into a decanter of oil he often traveled with and taken it just before going to a dinner meeting with a mysterious Mr. Drake, who hadn't been found.

Phoebe didn't know much about poisons or foraging, but something didn't sit right with her. She thought back to the card that she had found in Andreas' pocket. A chill passed over her. She stopped cleaning the basement and brought the broom upstairs.

She should get started on something. So she stirred up a bunch of eggs and put in milk and seasoning before popping it into a pan. Omelettes were just about the easiest thing to do, but Andreas never minded. Quickly, since the eggs were already cooking, she pulled a tomato out of the fridge and diced it before throwing it in. Tomatoes were very forgiving as ingredients. Barely cooked, they tasted fine. Well done, they tasted fine. She flipped the omelette and then sprinkled a little romano cheese on top.

She got out a plate and cut the omelette in half. She put a hand on her stomach. For some reason, she was having tons of dairy cravings, so she got out the ficelle that she had bought from the French bakery only a mile away from their house. She cut a small piece for herself and then got a bigger piece for Andreas. She got out her Kerrygold butter, an Irish butter that reminded her of French butter, and she slathered it all over the bread. The baby obviously wanted high calorie food.

The omelette halves were put into the sandwiches and then she cut up a cucumber to go on top for extra crunch. Andreas still wasn't home. She put in the smallest bit of mint inside of the sandwiches.

There. Perfect.

Andreas said that he would be home for lunch, but it was already later than she'd expect. She just knew that something was wrong. She couldn't put her finger on it, but Andreas had definitely been keeping something from her. Something definitely was wrong; there was something heavy in her gut.

She went to wash her hands. She opened up the fridge and got out a Coke. She knew that pregnant ladies weren't supposed to drink caffeine, but she needed the mix of caffeine and sugar right now.

"Hey, Phoebe."

Lunch Date

Phoebe

Phoebe whirled around, her heart racing a mile a minute.

"Oh, you're home."

He sniffed. "Is that mint?"

"I made omelette sandwiches."

"Smells pretty good." Andreas leaned down to kiss his wife. "You look more beautiful every day, you know that?"

Phoebe stood on her tiptoes to kiss him again. "I'm glad that you're home. I was starting to worry."

Andreas shook his head. "Why worry about a chef? What, do you think that one day you'll get called to the hospital to learn about my third degree burns? You think I'm going to chop off a finger or something?"

"No," Phoebe said. "You're right. It's silly to worry."

"Not silly," he said, tightening his arms around her. "I love that you care." He kissed her temple. "I'm starving. Let's sit down and eat."

Phoebe grabbed the plates so that they could eat at the table like civilized people. When they were done, she felt a lot better. Maybe all of those worries came from being a little too hungry. She was eating for two right now, after all, and maybe being extra hungry made her think crazy things. Andreas had nothing to do with that guy who was on TV. She ignored the strange feeling in her gut. It was probably just indigestion caused by the baby.

"I'm working the dinner shift tonight, babe. So don't wait up for me, okay?"

"Sounds good. I'm just going to clean up and then take a nap."

Andreas stood up and pulled Phoebe to her feet before lifting her by the waist and kissing her soundly.

"Go to bed early, okay? I want to wake you up...early, if you know what I mean."

She smiled and kissed his cheek. "I know what you mean."

He put her back on her feet.

"Love you."

"I love you, too." Phoebe sighed internally.

Andreas went back into his car and drove back to Chung's. Phoebe was exhausted, but she still cleaned up the pan that she'd used for the omelettes and the knife that she'd used for the butter. Finally, she did a quick wash of the plates that they had used.

She didn't feel as tired after washing the dishes. The strange feeling in her gut was still there. She didn't know too much about law enforcement, but she was the daughter of an FBI agent, after all, and her dad had taught her a few things over the years. Everything that he'd ever taught her was coming back in a flood now.

She snooped in all the usual hiding places: underwear drawers, under mattresses, secret drawers.

Nothing.

After finding exactly nada after her search, she gave up. Her husband had nothing to hide from her. These pregnancy hormones were really taking her for a ride.

She went to the TV room to settle on the couch and take a little day nap. As she closed her eyes, she remembered with a jolt that she hadn't turned off the TV downstairs.

Discovery

Phoebe

She got to her feet to turn it off before she could take her nap. She went straight to the TV and turned it off.

Had there always been a strange rectangle under the TV? It didn't look as if it were part of the original design. Phoebe touched the little box. She was surprised when a front panel swung forward to reveal a few buttons.

Phoebe pressed the green one and heard whirring behind her. Her heart was thumping in her chest when she saw something that she thought was a wall moving aside to show another room beyond it. She walked into the hidden room. At the far corner, there was an enormous safe that took up all the space from the ceiling to the floor. It had obviously been custom-built for this space. Maybe she had it backwards. Maybe the room was built for the safe.

She knew Andreas' password for everything: her birthday backwards. He told her that she was the most important thing in his life, and he'd never forget her birthday.

She spun the dial three times. She was shocked but not shocked when the safe came open. Inside, there was a black box. She pulled it out. Her eyes widened as she opened it. The box was filled with fake passports, tons of international currency, credit cards under many names, and a vial of liquid with some sort of white flower and onion-like buds popping out from the center on the label.

She started hyperventilating. Her heart was going a mile a minute, and her mind wasn't far behind. What did all of this mean?

Suddenly, she couldn't stand to be in the secret room for a second longer. She brought the black box up the stairs with her and put it on the counter.

Going into the pantry, she took

out the box of chamomile tea to soothe her nerves. She made just one cup and waited for the tea to steep as she paced around the kitchen, her mind going in circles.

She didn't know who her husband was. At all. It was clear that he was much more than she'd ever seen. She'd known that he had secrets, but then, who didn't?

Her eyes filled with tears that she refused to shed. She had to think about her baby. She could stay home and confront him, but she was afraid that he'd somehow convince her to stay.

Phoebe was done with the secrets. She dealt with enough from her dad.

Her daddy. He'd know what to do about this.

She gulped down her chamomile tea and washed out her tea cup. Phoebe opened up her MacBook and put up a vacation notice on her Etsy shop. She went upstairs and packed up some of her clothes and some toiletries into her biggest suitcase, lugging it downstairs to put it into the spacious trunk of her Lexus SUV. Before she had thought that it was a thoughtful wedding present, but she had to wonder now where Andreas had gotten the money. Was it clean?

She called her dad while she drove towards her childhood home, but he wasn't answering his phone. She left a message for him to meet her at their boathouse, which was her childhood hideout.

Phoebe saw that the needle of her fuel gauge was very close to empty, so she pulled into the nearest BP. She swiped her card and waited for her tank to fill up.

Her stomach grumbled suddenly. Apparently the buttery omelette sandwich wasn't enough for the baby.

"I'll feed you soon, I promise." She patted her baby. No matter what happened, she would never regret having a baby conceived in love, even if it turned out that the baby's father was something that she'd never even contemplated.

Throughout her pregnancy, she'd been Mrs. Waterworks, but she was very strangely calm. Maybe it was because she was operating under total shock. It would've been one thing if she'd seen that Andreas had some sort of secret life, probably a criminal one, but she had no idea. She loved Andreas completely. She knew that he was some kind of criminal, but she didn't really want to know more than that.

Her father had been right all along: Andreas' lack of family was definitely a symptom of a bigger problem. Maybe Andreas' criminal activity was a reason why he'd been late so often.

Finally, her tank was full. She replaced the handle where it belonged before closing the opening. She got a receipt from the gas pump, locked her car, and then headed towards the inside of the gas station with a really strong craving for Cheetos.

"Phoebe." A deep voice was speaking behind her. She turned and found a hand covering her mouth, muffling her screams as she lost consciousness.

Mansion

Phoebe

Phoebe woke up in the back of an SUV that was going through a winding driveway leading to a huge estate. She looked through the windows, but all she could see was a huge expanse of green in every direction, almost like a golf course. Her heart began to pound, but she needed to keep a grip on not freaking out. She was still clothed. Nothing had been done to her besides being knocked out. Her hands were free. She had to keep her head. It was a little too late now, but she wished that she'd taken self defense classes.

She told herself over and over to stay calm as the car pulled up to a very well-dressed man and two bodyguards in black at each side.

He opened her car door.

"Welcome, lovely Phoebe. You look prettier than the pictures. Won't you come in and eat?"

He asked as if she had a choice, which she didn't. Phoebe resisted the urge to put a hand on her baby. If she was lucky, this creep didn't know about the baby and wouldn't be able to use the baby as a bargaining chip.

"Of course," she said, keeping up with the pretense that she had a choice here. "I'd love to."

"Take my arm, dear."

Phoebe swallowed hard and then did as he asked. She hoped that he wouldn't hurt her, but she didn't have any control over the situation.

They walked inside of a very large house, a house big enough that she might call it a mansion.

"You're very beautiful, my dear. You look so much more like your mother than your father."

Phoebe swallowed hard again. How much did this guy know about her? Why was he talking about her parents?

They walked into a large dining room with two table settings that were beautifully done.

"I hope you don't mind a rustic meal, my dear. I don't stand on ceremony much. Just some pasta, if that's okay."

"Yes, I love pasta."

"Good, good."

Phoebe had the surreal experience of her kidnapper pulling her chair out for her and waiting for her to be seated before he took his own.

They ate quietly. Phoebe was expecting for there to be some kind of strange bitterness or any kind of indication of poison or drugs, but there wasn't anything besides normal fettucine alfredo.

When she was done, she wiped her mouth.

"Did you like it, dear Phoebe?"

Why did he insist on using

endearments? She'd never met him before. "It was delicious. Thank you."

"Oh, my chef deserves all the praise, but I'll pass it on. Would you like dessert?"

"No, thank you." Phoebe couldn't eat another bite. The serving had been more than generous.

"Then let's get down to a little business, shall we?"

"Business? I don't even know your name."

He hit the side of his head with his palm gently. "Oh, how rude. I'm Odhran Garin."

"Phoebe, but I know that you know that already."

He inclined his head just a smidgen. "Yes, I do." He cleared his throat. "My dear, do you know anything about the Crucible?"

Phoebe felt her eyebrows float upward.

"No."

He frowned at her and shook his head. "That's unfortunate."

Phoebe frowned back at him. What did he mean?

"Well, I should show you to your chambers, dear Phoebe."

He got to his feet and pulled out her chair. He put her hand on his arm again as he walked up a flight of steps. She got to the top-most floor of the mansion when he turned and brought her to a room.

"Here are your chambers. You should get some rest, dear Phoebe."

Strange. She was sleepy all the time now because of the baby, but being told to rest was weird.

Once inside of the room Odhran closed the door behind her. She was very startled to realize that there wasn't a door knob on the other side. She could hear the thunk of a deadbolt sliding. She was locked in with no way out.

There was a bathroom attached to her bedroom, so she would be okay for the moment.

Phoebe promised herself that she wouldn't cry. She sat down on the edge of her bed before falling backwards and staring at the ceiling. Her head was full of confusion. Odhran wanted some kind of

Crucible. Was this about her dad or her husband? Why was this guy being so polite and vague? Why was her lack of knowledge about the Crucible unfortunate?

Black Box

Andreas

When Andreas got home, the first thing he saw was the black box full of his passports. He felt like someone had punched him in the gut. She knew.

"Phoebe!" he called. "Baby, where are you?"

No answer.

He walked around the house, looking in the TV room where she liked to nap.

Then he went downstairs to the basement. He stared at the secret room. She'd seen the guns inside. He felt as if he might throw up, but he swallowed hard and forced it down.

Up in their bedroom, he found most of her toiletries gone and her closet mostly empty. Her huge suitcase, the one that he liked to tease her could house a family of five, was gone.

She couldn't have gone far, right? He tried to control his breathing to calm himself down as he went back downstairs to gather up his black box. It wasn't safe to leave that kind of thing just lying around. He put it back downstairs in his safe and locked all of it away again. It was safe enough, or it had been before his wife had found it. It'd have to do for now. He would find a new hiding place once he found his missing wife.

He walked back upstairs to hear his cell phone ringing. He rushed to where he'd left it on the countertop.

HAROLD KAINE said his caller ID. He might as well face the inevitable. He couldn't avoid her father. Phoebe was gone. He might need the old man's help to find her.

When Andreas hit accept, the first thing out of Mr. Kaine's mouth was, "What did you do?"

"Phoebe is missing."

"What?"

"Is she with you? I need to know that she's safe."

"She's not with me. She's not at home?"

"No."

He could hear Harold breathing hard over the phone.

"I want you to run a trace on her credit cards and phone, okay? We need to locate her last known location."

"Easy. I've had a trace on her for years."

Not a surprise. Andreas could hear tapping from the other end.

"The last time she used a credit card was at a gas station. Let's go." Harold rattled off the address of a BP station not too far away.

"I'll see you there."

Andreas hung up and got into his car, tapping the address into his GPS. He drove like the devil was behind him and parked in one of the parking spaces on the side of the gas station. As soon as he got out of his car, Harold was right there, and he grabbed his collar with both hands.

"What's going on?" Harold shouted into Andreas' face, his face red. "Where's my daughter?"

Andreas bit back his sharp retort. He knew that Harold was overwrought because Phoebe was missing.

"Please remove your hands from my collar."

Glaring, Harold loosened his grip and then finally let go.

"I knew you were trouble. I swear to God, if you've harmed one hair on her head…"

The moment was broken by

buzzing coming from Harold's phone.

Andreas watched Harold's face go from red to white.

"What's wrong?"

Harold held up his phone mutely.

Expect a call, Harold.

"Who wrote the text message?"

"Someone I wish I didn't know."

Harold went straight into the gas station. The kid behind the counter had milk-white skin, terrible acne, and blond dreads.

"Okay, kid, I want to see footage of the outside from the last four hours." Harold flashed his FBI badge at the kid.

"You're going to need a warrant for that." The kid stood up straighter. Andreas noticed that the kid's shirt had an image of a snake saying, "Don't Tread On Me." The boy was obviously libertarian. He might have very slender arms, but he also had a steel backbone.

"We should try something else. Call a judge, maybe." Andreas said it out loud so that the kid knew that they were taking him seriously. He watched the kid's chest puff out with pride.

Harold's cell phone rang. He walked out of the gas station before putting the phone on speaker.

"Daddy?"

"Phoebe? Baby girl, where are you?"

When there was no response, Harold said, "Honey, stay calm. We're going to find you."

But Phoebe wasn't talking anymore. An elegant, smooth voice came through the phone.

"Hello, Harold. You have something very precious of mine that I want. I want it back. I'm sure that you can relate."

Bath Kit

Phoebe

Phoebe must have fallen asleep, because she woke up in her bed. She found a bathrobe, new clothes, and a bath kit sitting on a chair in her room. Someone had come in while she was sleeping.

Phoebe tried to calm her nerves. Freaking out over the violation wasn't going to help her. She went into the shower with the bath kit to try to calm down. She knew that the stakes hadn't been raised beyond intimidation, though they'd definitely scared her — she was definitely shaken after the phone call that her captor placed to her father before she fell asleep. Was it yesterday or today? Phoebe couldn't tell. There weren't any clocks in her chambers.

She knew that Dad and Andreas were trying to find her, and she tried to take solace in that. They were both competent. They might be coming from opposite sides of the law, but between them, they should be able to find her. Phoebe had hope on her side.

She still cried in the shower, though. Her hormones and the baby made her sob quietly. What would happen if Odhran didn't get the Crucible, whatever it was?

The strong vanilla scent of the

bath soap was making her nauseous. She turned off the water so she could hurry out of the shower just in time to open her mouth and vomit into the toilet. She spat out the nasty taste in her mouth before going to the sink and rinsing her mouth out with water. She rummaged around under the sink for some mouthwash and used it to get rid of the taste.

Boat House

Andreas

Harold got into Andreas' car without a word, leaving his own car behind. It was a federal vehicle, and there'd be trouble if anybody stole it from the gas station. Andreas' car, a Tesla, was much faster in any case. Harold kept running his hand through his hair.

Andreas drove them back to the Kaines' house. They sat there in the driveway.

"You want to tell me what's going on? I want to know who took my wife." For once, Andreas wasn't the one in the hot seat. He wasn't taking too much pleasure in it, but he didn't have time for the normal games that he played with Phoebe's father. "What does this guy want?"

Harold rubbed his face. "Too many people will get hurt."

Andreas was pretty sure that it was exactly what he'd found when he was researching Harold, but he needed confirmation. Gritting his teeth, Andreas cleared his throat. He didn't want to respond to Harold. His wife and child were more important than faceless strangers. When he could speak civilly again, he said, "My wife and child could get hurt if you don't talk, Harold. Tell me what's happening."

The men locked eyes for a moment. For the first time, Andreas could see a glimmer of respect in Harold's eyes.

Harold's hands flew to his head. "We should talk in the boat house. I've kept my wife away from everything that I do for this long. I'm not going to start getting her involved now, even with my daughter at stake."

"Where is it?"

"It's about an acre away from the house."

They got out of Andreas' car and went straight to the boat house at a jog.

"I hope my wife doesn't see us."

Andreas thought that it was

strange that Harold was so concerned about appearances at the moment, but he understood the motivation to keep his wife away from the dirt that he got involved in.

"Where do you think that she could be?" They both went inside of the boat house, which had heating and cooling. The two of them took off their coats and put them on the coat rack by the door.

"When I had my people run a search for her, we realized that her cell phone was off of the grid. The last known location is that damned gas station."

"So the trail is cold?"

"I didn't say that."

"But there aren't any other

leads?"

Harold stuttered for a minute, then he changed his mind. "That's right."

"What's the precious thing that he wants?"

"I can't talk about it."

"Are you joking? Fuck the fibbies. This is Phoebe we're talking about. Your daughter, you know? What kind of father doesn't ride to his child's safety when he has the key for her release?" Andreas closed his eyes and ended his rant. In a much calmer voice, he asked, "What can you tell me? Any information that you have is going to help on my end."

"What end is that?" Harold looked at Andreas. "I knew that you weren't really a chef."

"Are you even being real right now? You're not really in a position to judge right now. Tell me what Phoebe's kidnapper wants."

"I can't even discuss it."

Andreas punched the wall, breaking through the drywall.

"I'll pay for a contractor. Listen, even if you don't want to give this thing away, you've got to give me enough information for me to pretend to give it to him. I can trick him into thinking that we're coming to deliver it. I can extract Phoebe by myself, but I need to know where she is. Who is the smug bastard who has her?"

"I need booze." Harold went to the corner of the boat house. He got out two cold bottles of beer with twist-off caps. He threw one at Andreas, who caught it in one hand.

Harold opened up his beer and took a swig.

"I never liked you, you know. Not for a second."

Andreas didn't give a damn. He knew that it stressed Phoebe out, but he couldn't care less about what her old man thought of him.

Harold took another sip of his beer. "I know that you obviously love her. That's why I let you two marry."

Andreas held back a snort. Harold Kaine couldn't have stopped their marriage. Andreas would've taken her away before that ever happened.

"You get some points for loving her. She deserves that, you know? My baby girl deserves the best." Harold drained the rest of the bottle quickly, chugging all the beer down like a frat boy. "I should've stocked something stronger."

"Tell me what I need to know."

"Do you know about the levels of information in the federal government? Sensitive, confidential, secret, top secret, and then levels that I've never even heard of."

"What does that have to do with anything?"

"What I'm about to tell you is sensitive, not confidential exactly. If you had an infinite amount of time, you could piece together the picture from old documents and newspaper articles."

Andreas bit back his retort. He wanted to tell Mr. Kaine to get to the point, but exploding again wouldn't serve any purpose. He could see that Mr. Kaine was very close to telling him what was going on.

"I need you to reassure me that this information won't get into the wrong hands."

Andreas looked Mr. Kaine in the eyes. "It won't."

Harold tossed his empty beer bottle into a blue recycling bin. Andreas bit his tongue, wanting to shake the old man. He was completely on edge and ready to save his wife, if only he knew where she was.

He wasn't expecting Mr. Kaine to walk out of the boat house.

Copying the ID

Andreas

Andreas quickly reached into his pocket to pull out his smartphone. He had a way of storing encrypted images and videos, and he opened up the custom app that had been specially designed for the Agency.

Reaching into Mr. Kaine's coat to get his wallet, he then took out his FBI ID and took a clear image of it with his phone, using a special attachment that didn't look like much to scan the RFID as well.

He had barely put the ID back into Mr. Kaine's wallet and put the whole thing back into his pocket when Mr. Kaine walked back into the boat house.

"What I'm about to do is treason, do you understand?"

"Phoebe," Andreas reminded him.

Harold nodded. "Phoebe." He gave him a small blue folder. Andreas opened it and could see that Harold took out some documents before he brought the file to Andreas. There were neat blue tabs that were numbered down the side, and some of the tabs were missing.

He quickly scanned the contents of the file. It was just a bunch of numbers with redacted names. There was some kind of engineering consulting company that all the money was paid into. The biggest customer's name wasn't there, but his bank was listed. It stood out like a sore thumb among the big American banks on the list. This guy had his bank accounts in the Caymans. Andreas wasn't big on the white collar side of things, but he wasn't stupid. He knew people who could trace this kind of thing. With the right hacker, he knew that he could trace the transaction amounts and dates and come up with names.

Andreas closed the folder. "Thank you very much. Could you wait for me before you make a move? I'm going to do a little research and find the guy who has Phoebe."

Harold put his hand over his

eyes. "I...I'm a law enforcement agent. I don't want to know what you're about to do, but I want you to get my daughter back. Is that clear?"

"I understand."

Harold took his hand away from his eyes. "I should go check on Sally...she's probably noticed your car in the driveway. I'll have her help me go back to the gas station. I'll be back in a minute."

Harold went back towards the house, which gave Andreas enough time to pull his phone out a second time and take pictures of every page of the file that Harold had given him. When he saw Harold walking back towards the boat house, he slipped his phone back into his pocket.

"Sally will take me back to my car. Are we done here?" Harold asked.

"Yes."

"Give me the file."

Andreas nodded, although if he hadn't had the foresight to take pictures of all of the information, it would've been utterly useless to just see it once. "Okay."

Harold's shoulders relaxed just a smidgen when he took back the file. Andreas knew that it had been compiled off the books, and therefore wasn't exactly under the FBI's purview, but giving information to someone he knew was a criminal was definitely hard for Mr. Kaine. Andreas needed to create that distance between them so that whatever mud Andreas got into didn't splash on Phoebe's parents.

"I'll check back with you late tomorrow with whatever I've found by then."

"Meet at the nearest Starbucks?"

Andreas knew which one he was talking about. The nearest Starbucks was within easy walking distance of the house.

"Yup." Mr. Kaine still wanted to protect his wife from what was going on. Mrs. Kaine wouldn't be worried about Phoebe being out of contact for a few days, but if it turned into a few weeks, she'd panic. Andreas needed to prevent that from ever happening.

Dimitri

Andreas

Andreas got back into his car and only ran one loop to throw off any tails that he might've picked up before he headed for his hacker's domain. Andreas and Phoebe lived in Springfield, well within the DC metro area but close-ish to her parents who lived near Quantico. Mr. Kaine was an old dog and didn't do much active case work on the ground anymore. He got pulled to teach unarmed defense tactics; Andreas knew that in a fair fight, he'd want Mr. Kaine at his back, even if the man hated his guts. They both loved Phoebe, and they knew that if either of them did anything to the other, they'd pay for it a hundred times over.

Andreas knocked on the door of a small one-story house. The house was unassuming, but the magic happened downstairs. He didn't know how his hacker explained the enormous power use of all of the supercomputers that they had plugged in here, but nobody had come to shut them down yet.

Andreas saw a camera swivel towards him.

"Andreas?"

"It's me."

Dimitri buzzed him in without another word.

Andreas went into the door and made sure that it was closed and locked behind him. Dimitri's house was as safe as you could get in the suburbs, but it would be stupid to get shut down because you forgot to close a door. Andreas didn't make stupid mistakes. He only made ones of huge magnitude, like falling in love with the daughter of an FBI agent who totally hated him.

"Why are you here?"

"I need you to trace some bank transactions."

"Yeah? Over $10,000?"

"Safely over $10,000." Banks were required to report any transactions over $10,000 to the FDIC to help it keep an eye on money laundering. If you had access to their database, then you could see the movement of money throughout the American economy. Andreas took his cell phone out of his pocket and switched to images.

"You have exact dollar amounts and dates? And the bank?" Dimitri looked like Christmas had come early. "Piece of cake."

"I certainly hope so."

Dimitri took the phone from Andreas and set it in front of him as his hands moved over his keyboard so fast that they blurred. Andreas knew that Dimitri liked his Dvorak keyboard because of the 50% increased efficiency, but it was definitely weird and ergonomic.

"Done."

"Seriously?"

Dimitri pretended to dust off his knuckles. "I'm fast."

"You're the best, Dimitri."

Andreas watched Dimitri preen a little bit. He knew that it wasn't the easiest thing to be a computer genius who spent most of his time in his basement, and Andreas also knew that Dimitri didn't hang around the kind of people who praised him for his work. Andreas made a mental note to try to do it more often.

He looked at the windows that Dimitri had pulled up on his six-screen array.

"Weapons ring?"

"They aren't just guns. They're

much more than that. They can take out small cities or very large urban neighborhoods. They could take out L'Enfant Plaza if they wanted to. The Pentagon is a little better protected, but shutting down L'Enfant Plaza would definitely be within their power."

"And one of the weapons in question is missing."

"The worst one. It has five times the power of the closest one."

Andreas whistled. "That's a lot of firepower."

"The FBI has no clue how it lost track of that particular weapon."

Andreas wondered if Mr. Kaine had taken the weapon and hidden it, but no, that didn't add up. Mr. Kaine was so squeaky clean that he practically glowed with lemony freshness. He wasn't the sort of guy — Harold Kaine wasn't going to hide the transmitter for a series of bombs planted across the Southern US for kicks, a price, or any other reason. Mr. Kaine was definitely in danger, though, that much was for certain. The people who lost an absolute ton of money during his raid would want the weapon back.

"Is that everything?"

"That's what I can get with the information that isn't redacted. Whoever you pulled that file from didn't want us to be able to find much."

"Yeah, I know." He couldn't help

but wonder what exactly Harold Kaine had hidden from him when his daughter's life was at stake.

"I've got to go to Chung's. Thanks, man." Andreas slapped Dimitri on the back. It was useful to keep him on retainer. Andreas didn't need a superb hacker all the time, but when he did, he wanted the best.

"Anytime, Andreas." One of the reasons why Dimitri was so fantastic was because he didn't ask questions. He didn't know if Dimitri's real name was Dimitri or not, and he didn't care. Andreas still went by his birth name, but he'd had so many that he'd lost track. Once he fulfilled his contract for the Agency, he was going to stick to being Andreas.

Andreas went upstairs and got into his car to head straight for the restaurant. Chung didn't normally get his hands too dirty, but Andreas knew that he had a good touch with any kind of paperwork. There were rumors that Chung was involved with some white collar stuff, and Andreas was about to find out whether or not that was true.

Copy

Andreas

When Andreas got to the restaurant, he parked his car into his normal spot around the back.

"Andreas? What are you doing here? I wasn't expecting you today." Chung was wearing an apron.

"Business good?"

"Yeah."

"I need your help with something. Tracing some transactions..."

"Do you know which bank it's through?"

"Some bank that has Cayman at the beginning."

"I didn't know that you were involved in that kind of thing. I thought you just did some...ah...wet work." They both knew that Andreas was a gun man, primarily, but it wouldn't do to openly discuss it out in the back of the restaurant.

"We should get inside."

Chung and Andreas walked into the restaurant's kitchen before going into a backroom.

"Give me a minute." Andreas watched as Chung used his thumbprint to boot up a huge computer that was connected to a gigantic monitor.

Andreas fought the urge to bite his nails, a habit that had been beaten out of him at a young age. His eyes flicked to the clock on the wall. Time was ticking fast. He needed to find Phoebe as soon as he possibly could. He didn't want to think about the worst case scenario. If her kidnapper meant to hurt Phoebe, it was already done and Andreas was powerless to stop it. Whomever had made that phone call could have given a violent incentive, but that didn't mean that it wouldn't be escalated to that level if they didn't follow through with the missing weapon.

Andreas watched as Chung's screen filled with the big word BLOCKED in red letters.

Something had to give. Andreas banged his fist on the table enough to make him bite a curse. He leaned back in his chair and crossed his arms, fuming. Drawing in a breath, he pulled his phone out of his pocket and opened the photo gallery.

Passing the phone over to Chung, he asked, "Can you replicate this?"

Chung's brows drew together. "Have we met?" Chung's reputation, the shadowy one that Andreas wasn't sure of, was confirmed. He knew that Chung did any paperwork...

"How long?"

"One hour. Two, tops."

"I need a meeting with Ezra, too."

Chung drew in a breath.

"I'm pretty reasonable, but you know what Ezra costs." It wasn't quite his firstborn, but it was pretty close.

"It's fine. I can handle it."

Scary

Phoebe

Phoebe heard a knock on her door.

"I was wondering if you'd like to take a stroll in the garden?"

"Yes." Phoebe would handle his presence if she didn't have to stare at the wall of her bedroom.

She heard the door being unlocked. The slick, elegant man was standing outside of her bedroom. "Excellent."

He took her arm again, and Phoebe wondered if he was trying to prevent her from running away by basically keeping in constant contact with her. They went down the stairs until they got out of the house. Phoebe looked at the big wall that ran all the way around the property and groaned. Escaping wouldn't be very easy. There was barbed wire across the top, which definitely spoiled the look but would prevent her from climbing a wall and going over.

Now they were outside of a greenhouse. Odhran opened it up by twisting the doorknob. "I have a special affinity for carnivorous plants. They smell very sweet."

Phoebe walked with him through the greenhouse that contained dozens upon dozens of carnivorous plants. She almost gagged from the sickly sweet smell of decay. Carnivorous plants didn't smell good at all. They screamed of blood money spent with the ego of a self-made king who cut his way through the competition.

"You know, some carnivorous plants are large enough to eat rodents. Or pieces of meat. Would you like to feed one?"

Phoebe suppressed a shudder. "No, thank you."

"A shame." She watched him turn to a small bloody bowl and toss a piece of meat into a big carnivorous plant. "This is a pitcher plant with a capacity of approximately 2 liters."

"Fascinating." Phoebe's skin was crawling. She didn't want to be in a greenhouse full of plants that could eat her. The message that he was sending was unmistakable. He could afford expensive plants and he was powerful enough to keep them all going.

She didn't know where her impulse control was when she asked, "When can I go home?"

His eyes changed shade from a pale green to a dark grey, as if he had a thunderstorm inside. He locked eyes with her.

"Will you indulge me in some of your dancing? I know that you've done ballet and modern. I've been told that you're quite something to see. I'll have a costume delivered to your room."

He hadn't answered her question at all, and now her stomach felt weird because he'd asked her to dance.

"Do I really have a choice here?"

He laughed and his eyes switched back to green. "It's polite to ask. Let's go back to your room. I'll tell my staff to put a costume in your room." She watched as he tapped on his smart watch. "It should be there by the time that we get back."

Phoebe understood now how much menace lay beneath the surface. His tone about the costume being there soon was very mild, but it was just too mild. Whatever Odhran Garin wanted, he would get.

Phoebe fought the urge to put a protective hand on her stomach. It was better if he didn't know about the baby.

Odhran walked her slowly and courteously back into the house. They walked all the way back up the stairs to Phoebe's bedroom.

"I'll expect you downstairs in ten minutes." Odhran closed her door but didn't lock it. For a short time, she had some privacy.

As he had told her, there was a costume lying on the bed. It was a purple and black dress. The inner panel was purple with some kind of flowers all over it, and the black parts were on the outer thirds of the garment to create a silhouette like that knockout Stella McCartney color contour dress that Kate Winslet had caused a sensation in.

She took off the clothes that he had given to her before and put on the dress. She gasped when she looked in the mirror and saw how sheer the purple fabric was when it was on her body. It was nearly transparent. She had tulle on her dance outfits, of course, but always with something beneath it.

She looked around her room for hidden passages or covered vents. Anything at all would help. If she could hide herself somewhere on the compound, she was pretty sure that she could find a way out...or at least she'd be able to figure something out when night fell. Maybe she'd be able to hitchhike her way out.

She really wished that she had taken self defense classes. Her father had taught her the bare basics, but it had bored her.

Looking back into the mirror, she touched her slightly rounded stomach. But she had to quickly move her hand, because she didn't know if there were cameras in her room. She had to get the baby out of here.

Oregano

Phoebe

When Phoebe got downstairs, the door to the dining room was open and she could smell oregano wafting out.

"Come in, come in," Odhran said, standing up as she approached. "Eat something before your dance."

"What is here?"

"A filet mignon with mashed sweet potatoes. You deserve the best." Like the day before, he pulled her chair out before she sat down. Having him so close to her made her flesh crawl.

He sat across from her.

"Dig in." He seemed a little less polite than he had been before, and Phoebe didn't know whether or not that was a good sign or not. Ever since she asked when she could leave, he'd been just a little colder, as if she had disrespected him by reminding him that she wasn't at his home of her own accord. Maybe Odhran was one of those types who needed to think that his presence was awesome and overrode the fact that he kidnapped people and held them against their will.

She looked at the steak knife next to her plate and then at Odhran. Odhran immediately rang a bell by pressing a button under the table.

"Please cut Ms. Phoebe's meat for

her, Eric, then take away the knife."

"Of course, sir." Eric was wearing a chef's whites. He pulled the plate away from Phoebe and cut everything into small pieces before giving it back to her.

"I hope you enjoy, miss." Phoebe couldn't be mad at him for doing what his employer asked.

Odhran was smiling. Phoebe totally hated him in that moment. He was toying with her. He'd probably asked for steak just to torment her with a tiny bit of hope.

Phoebe stabbed each piece of food as if she totally hated it, but she had to admit that his chef was phenomenal. The filet mignon wasn't anything like any steak she'd had before, even at the fancier restaurants in DC.

When her plate was empty, her stomach was groaning.

"Done, my dear?"

She wasn't his dear, but she responded anyway. "Yes, thank you."

"So now it's time for a performance."

Phoebe's hackles rose. Who was he to casually command her to give a performance? She wasn't on his payroll, and she didn't take anything from him. She opened her mouth to speak, but seeing the smile on his lips, she closed her mouth.

Something told her that refusing him would be extremely unwise. She couldn't reveal that she was pregnant and a little bit delicate at the moment. Phoebe closed her eyes for a minute as her panic rose. She knew several low-impact routines. She'd stick to those, and the baby would be fine.

She hoped.

Dancing for a private audience was demeaning and made her feel like a stripper — and she was sure that Odhran wanted to make her uncomfortable. But she was between a rock and a hard place. If she weren't pregnant, she'd take some bigger risks and just run for it. But she was pregnant, and she wouldn't ever do anything that would endanger her baby.

Something told her that he was

five steps ahead of her, anyway. He brought her to a banquet room full of ornate decor that reminded her of her first visit to Versailles. The rich detailing was overly ornate.

"On the center platform, please."

Dancing

Phoebe

Phoebe felt more like a stripper than ever as she went to the raised platform. It wasn't a stage, not a real one. She had an attack of nausea, but she didn't want to show it.

She looked down at Odhran. He was perfectly smug and looked like he was totally entitled to whatever dancing she did.

Someone dimmed the lights and started music as if it were a real performance. She closed her eyes and centered herself before doing the motions of a routine that she'd done when she was fifteen for several performances. She smiled as she remembered how full of fire she'd been as a teenager.

When had that changed? Maybe when she grew up and became an adult and caught just a glimpse of the world that her father had protected her from for so long. And it was her way of flipping the bird to Odhran, who thought that he could control her. She was complying with his request, but her way.

At the climax of the dance, when there were a lot of leaps, she was very careful with her landings, not jumping as high as she really could. She was hyper-conscious of the angles of this part of the dance to ensure the safety of her child.

Then it was at an end. She gracefully curtsied to the audience of one.

She heard Odhran clapping and gritted her teeth before replacing her grimace with a fake smile, a performer's lie. If anything, she'd been taught to pretend as if she enjoyed performing, even when she was sick, even when she was tired, even when she felt as if she might throw up any moment.

"Excellent. I could watch it a thousand times. Do it again."

Phoebe swallowed the vomit that threatened to spill. The music started yet again. She felt as if she were a puppet whose strings he was pulling.

She was sure that it was intentional. He wanted to show her that he had absolute power over her actions; she was his marionette.

"Cut the music."

What? What did Odhran want?

"I changed my mind about your costume. I want you in a ball gown."

Phoebe felt more like his doll than ever. She couldn't stop the flash of anger that crossed her face.

"You should wear my colors. Let's get you a purple gown, so you match my guards. Someone will help you backstage."

Phoebe turned around. She was in the center of the room. What kind of backstage was there?

She turned and saw a guard

behind her. He picked her up off of the stage and threw her over his shoulder. She was instantly concerned about the baby in her stomach, which was in contact with the guard's shoulder.

"We use a back room as our backstage area." From the guard's tone, she surmised that the concept of kidnapping girls and forcing them to perform was an everyday occurrence for Chez Odhran.

There was another man who had a purple dress in his hands.

"We have a folding screen. Hurry. He doesn't like to wait." She saw that the costumer's hands were shaking. This whole thing affected more than just her.

She took the dress from his hands and quickly went behind the folding screen. She quickly stepped into it. She looked for the silver lining. The dress definitely covered more than the first costume, but she was worried about just how far Odhran was ready to go. What would happen if she couldn't find a way out or Andreas and her dad couldn't free her?

She should've just stayed at home and confronted Andreas about the black box. If she had, she wouldn't be some rich creep's ballerina doll.

It was funny how much the shock of finding out that Andreas was some kind of criminal had passed when she was kidnapped. She was still totally astounded by him keeping fake passports, international currency, guns, and everything else in their house. She thought that their marriage was honest and close. But she wasn't sure just whom she had married.

But she should've given him a chance to explain before running off.

"Are you done? He's asking for you."

Phoebe glared at the voice, even though it wasn't his fault. She could hear the nervousness in the costumer's voice. She didn't think that he was here by choice. Odhran just pulled people that he wanted to work on his estate in, and he didn't care about what they wanted.

The costumer was terrified, and Phoebe knew that the depth of his terror had to be due to being punished before. Phoebe got out because she had no desire to learn how Odhran disciplined any errant "employees." Her initial fear was turning into pure loathing for his mind games.

"Ready." Phoebe raised her chin and went back into the room where she had performed earlier.

Not Gourmet

Andreas

"What? No fancy gourmet food?"

Andreas had a bag of carry-out from Chung's. Mr. Kaine didn't know that it was just a cover.

"Nope, just some simple beef lo mein. Not really in the mood to cook something gourmet tonight."

"You aren't any closer than you were before you left?" He coughed. "And beef lo mein is just fine. Sally likes it."

Mr. Kaine and Andreas ate in the boat house, which was as well furnished as a very small guest house. He could see why Phoebe had spent time there as a kid.

"You know, Phoebe or Sally disappearing is my worst nightmare. It's the thing that I've been the most worried about since I started at the FBI. I know that you think that I should be breaking more rules, but my job is everything that I have left. I'm trying to uphold my oath. It's the hardest decision that I've ever faced, but giving into Odhran's pressure could mean the death of hundreds or thousands just to start."

"Odhran has a bomb?" Andreas wanted to confirm what exactly the Crucible was.

Grimacing, Harold said, "It's much more than a bomb." He got to his feet. "I'm going to carry this delicious beef lo mein up to my wife while it's still hot."

Andreas waited until he was gone to go straight for Harold's coat. He must've worn it back out here after he went to pick up his car. His wallet was in the same place that Andreas had found it before: his right pocket. Harold was right-handed, so it made sense. Andreas whipped out the fake that he had Chung print from his image of Harold's FBI badge with the right RFID. Using the edge of his shirt to prevent any fingerprints staying on it, he wiped the prints before putting Harold's badge back where it belonged. Chung could definitely handle something like this, and

Harold's now fake badge could probably get him in.

Andreas put Harold's real badge into his own wallet in a little pocket that would block the signal until he wanted to take it out. He could access all the FBI's databases now and get some real answers. If Harold was flagged, he'd have a real excuse: he'd been pick-pocketed, and he had the fake ID to prove it.

Painting

Phoebe

"Wake up." Phoebe opened one eye. The stress of dancing for Odhran last night had made her sleep deeply, despite her fear.

"What time is it?"

"Five AM." Odhran was far too cheerful for Phoebe. "You're going to sit for a painter."

"What?"

"You'll need to change into this." Odhran was holding a mesh nightgown in his hands. There was a glint of malice in his eyes and she knew that he wasn't a patient man.

He had forced her to dance again and again and again until her limbs shook and her whole body was soaked with perspiration. The ball gown had covered her up better, yeah, but it was stifling. She had sweated like crazy. He finally called a halt when she thought that she was going to faint right there on the stage.

It chilled her to think that he might think of doing more to her than he already had. She knew that she had to get out of his estate in any way that she could as fast as she could.

Somehow.

She went into her bathroom for a semblance of privacy and got into the sheer mesh gown.

When she got out, there was someone else in the room, a slender older man who had an easel set up in the corner. She didn't know if he had been there the whole time and she hadn't noticed him or if he'd come in just moments before.

"Just sit on the bed. This painting is a gift for your father."

Phoebe's blood turned to ice.

Why would he want to deliver a painting when he could just deliver her? Was this part of his game, or was it some kind of sick warning?

A long time later, Phoebe was pressing her lips together by the time the painter had completed a painting that Odhran liked.

"Beautiful," Odhran said, his eyes

going to Phoebe's curves. "Your dear daddy will like this."

Phoebe knew better than to ask why her father would like it.

The painter and Odhran finally left her alone in her room. She heard the click of the lock.

Phoebe felt her lips quiver as her tears were finally allowed to come out. She practically ripped off the strange mesh gown off of her when she was alone, and went into the shower to wash away things that soap couldn't. She began to sob inside of the shower and wrapped her arms around herself. She'd been hopeful throughout this whole nightmare, but he was raising the stakes of the mind game. She couldn't bear the thought of being touched by Odhran if that was his next play, since she'd been asked to dress in overly revealing clothing.

She thought about the baby. She was lucky that she wasn't showing yet.

Footsteps were heard outside of her door. She held her breath, her eyes wide, nearly hyperventilating as they came closer and closer to her door. Then the footsteps went away. What in the world was that about? Did he come here to…and then change his mind? She curled her body into a ball, sure that she wouldn't feel safe in her prison any longer. Odhran was totally unpredictable. She had no idea when

Andreas or her dad would find her. Even the FBI had blind spots...and she had no idea what Andreas was involved with.

Researching

Andreas

Andreas couldn't get comfortable when he lay down to sleep that night. He was staying in the boat house to keep close to the Kaines until Phoebe was found. He kept thinking of worst-case scenarios. It was karma; he'd hurt enough people to know just what humans were capable of. His hands weren't clean. He thought of Phoebe on the other end of the things that he'd done in the name of the Agency, and he couldn't fall asleep. When he closed his eyes, he saw Phoebe on the other end of his knife.

He got out of bed when it was clear that he wasn't going to get much sleep tonight. He should look more deeply into the engineering company that they had found. He pulled out a laptop.

Going right to their corporate press releases, there were press releases about military applications for several of their products. He kept clicking through them. The average American didn't pay much attention to defense; it was taken care of for them. But many of the government's biggest defense contractors were publicly traded, which meant that some of their information was available to a casual observer.

And Andreas was much more

than that.

His head began to pound as the hours ticked by, but he ignored it. He needed to figure out what exactly the Crucible was so he could save Phoebe. It was the key to getting his wife back where she belonged.

He needed to come clean to her, but he'd have to find her first.

Rubbing his eyes, he noticed that he'd gone through an enormous amount of pages, learning more about large-scale weapons than he ever wanted. He was tempted to access the FBI from his laptop, but he needed to wait for a better place to go. He knew just where he was going to go with Harold's card. Together, they could get the information that he needed to find his wife.

His phone rang.

"Hello?"

"You asleep?"

Andreas rubbed his eyes. "No."

"We've got the green light for a meeting."

"Roger."

Chung hung up. The information that he'd needed to convey was there.

* * *

The next morning, Andreas had already finished his eggs and was ready to grab his coat to go out.

Mr. Kaine's phone rang, and he looked at Andreas, who froze right where he was. He said a prayer of thanks that Mrs. Kaine was still asleep.

It rang again. Mr. Kaine put the phone on speaker and mute at the same time.

"Good morning, Harold. What a lovely day, isn't it? Your daughter is a very beautiful dancer. You've definitely placed me in a tempting position."

"If you lay a hand on her..."

Odhran cut him off. "Don't worry. I'm not planning on giving into my primal impulses. She's not my enemy. She's pretty useless when it comes to information, which is the most precious currency, as you know. I need you to give me what I want."

"Take me instead."

Andreas' eyes popped open. Was

Mr. Kaine offering what he thought he was?

"That's all I can give."

"Fair enough." Odhran paused. "We can make the trade at a park near The Pentagon. They block all the signals around there, so it's definitely ideal. I'll text you the meeting time and exact location."

Harold hit the red button on his phone to hang up. His face was so white that Andreas wondered if he should ask him to sit down.

"I think I know where she is."

"Where?"

Satellites

Andreas

Harold had given him an address, and Andreas had taken his laptop to Chip's to get a secure connection when he hacked the FBI. The ID worked perfectly to unlock the door. He used the satellites to check for weak points on the estate, but he couldn't find anything. Whoever was in charge of the security of the estate was very good. There wasn't any way to just march in and grab his wife without setting off a bunch of alarms.

Sighing, he drank a sip of Chip's coffee, choking it down for the caffeine. He changed the coordinates of the satellites. If Harold wound up in this thug's hands, he might not make it out if he planned on being a martyr, a hero. Sighing, he sat back, seeing his screen but not reading it.

His mind ran the different scenarios. The outcome for Mr. Kaine would be pretty grim. He cleared his history and closed his laptop.

"The cookie you requested, sir." Andreas looked up at the barista, who had a plain package wrapped in brown paper.

"Thank you for my cookie."

Andreas tossed his coffee in the trash and headed for the back rooms at Chip's. When he was in one of the small offices, he opened the package up. It was a layout of the underground tunnels at Odhran's estate. There was an area that was highlighted, the second part of the same mission. They wanted him to go into the estate and get whatever they'd highlighted. This couldn't be connected to the first mission to take out Harold Kaine, could it?

He raised an eyebrow. What was going on? Did they mean for Harold Kaine to sacrifice himself and kill two birds with one stone?

He wasn't sure if they were giving a way out of stone-cold murdering his father-in-law. The layout didn't actually show any accessible doors or passages leading from any level into the house itself. Memorizing the layout, tracing with his finger several routes through the estate, he sighed. He knew that it still wasn't going to be easy. Andreas needed to get his wife first; the retrieval was secondary. He hoped that he could do both.

He only had one more job after this one. He was almost done.

Exchange

Andreas

The next day, the ride to the estate was incredibly tense. Harold and Andreas hadn't spoken for the entire ride as both of them were suffering from a chaos of thoughts. Was the exchange the right thing to do?

At least they were doing something. Andreas hadn't told Mr. Kaine about his secondary mission. Harold hadn't talked much about this decision. The retrieval of the object wasn't all that important. Phoebe and her father were a thousand times more important than anything he needed to do for the Agency's sake.

He was going to lay down his life for his daughter's. Andreas understood and respected the sacrifice; if it came down to it, he'd do the same thing for Phoebe's sake. He was just much less valuable than an FBI agent. It was a necessary sacrifice, although Andreas wished that he didn't have to play it that way. But he would do his best to make sure that the Kaines were safe.

Andreas parked in an empty cornfield.

"Text if you get a call."

They exchanged a meaningful glance.

"I'll be back."

Harold nodded but said nothing at all, not even, "Good luck." For a man about to die and/or be tortured, it fit.

Managing a grim smile, Andreas stepped out and let the door slam behind him. He needed to get to the tunnels.

He didn't envy Harold, sitting alone in the car. He didn't know what he'd told his wife, but Andreas was not looking forward to going back to his mother-in-law without his father-in-law.

He headed to a small shack that concealed an entrance to the underground tunnels. Harold thought that Andreas was going to be helping Phoebe out; he had no idea that

Andreas was going to be on the estate, too.

He followed the track that the Agency had highlighted on the blueprint, passing a small waterfall. The estate was built around a small valley, but the tunnels radiated beyond the valley. It was probably an ideal setup for smuggling.

He was relieved that there didn't seem to be any cameras detected by his bug finder. It made sense, if they were this close to The Pentagon. He shook his head. The Pentagon was so careful to protect its own secrecy that it ended up concealing the people that it was afraid of.

He hurried through the first two tunnels until he reached the third one and took a glance around, looking at all the corners. There hadn't seemed to be any direct entrances into the house on the map, not even a ventilation system that would bring him upwards.

Frowning, he turned his attention to the circled area on the map. It was a picture of the Grand Canyon in a frame. There had to be something besides that, which suggested that the Agency had some kind of contact and could have helped him way more than they actually had.

He wound his way through the tunnels until he got to the painting. There was a small flash drive in the frame. He put it in his pocket.

He ran back, knowing that he

shouldn't leave Harold stewing there for too long. When he got back to the car, one look told him that Odhran had already called.

Harold looked as if he had looked death in the face.

"Let's hurry up and drive there. We've got an hour to wait." He was pale, but Andreas respected him for keeping it together.

Drawing in a sharp breath, Andreas looked forward as the car lurched to life and headed towards the rendezvous point. He felt as if he had failed Harold, but there weren't any entrances leading from the tunnels into the estate. He would've been pushing his luck to try the other tunnels, not knowing what kind of surveillance might be on the other paths. Phoebe was his priority, not Harold.

Andreas' heart was tight in his chest when they finally got to the rendezvous point. He could see Phoebe in the back seat. She glared at him as the car came to a stop, avoiding his eyes after that.

A goon pulled her out of the car.

"Baby girl, you okay?"

"I'm okay, Daddy." She was crying. "You should leave now. I'm okay." They all knew that Harold wouldn't be.

"Too late, baby girl." Harold turned to her captors. "Let her go, okay? I'm ready to take her place."

Harold sounded cool and

collected, but Andreas could see the sweat on Harold's forehead.

Odhran got out of the car and grinned at Harold. It was a terrifying grin, the kind that suggested that he had all kinds of sadistic plans for Harold.

Phoebe was frowning at Odhran.

"Dear Phoebe, you better walk towards the handsome guy. Go on, now."

She could've killed with her eyes from her laser glare.

Odhran's grin deepened. He motioned at Harold to start moving, too. He didn't say to not try anything stupid. Harold was so honorable that he'd just go like a lamb to slaughter.

Andreas reached out for Phoebe

when she came close. She flinched away from him. What had Odhran done to her?

"Daddy!" Phoebe turned around to call out to her father just in time to see one of the thugs knock her dad out with a single blow to the jaw.

When she would've run to him, Andreas wrapped his arms around his wife.

"Baby, we've got to get going."

"Daddy!" she screamed again.

Andreas pulled his wife into the car.

"We have to get out of here."

"They...they have my dad."

"I know, sweetheart."

"Don't call me that. I don't even know you."

"I think that we have more important things to do right now than throw around accusations, okay? We've got to figure out a way to get your dad back."

Phoebe tried to open her door. Andreas put the car in park to calm her down.

"No, Phoebe." She hit him with her fists, landing on his chest. He gathered her closer.

"Phoebe, you better calm down. I promise you that we'll get your father back. Calm down, okay? You're stressing out the baby."

She was crying in earnest now. "Turn the car around and get my daddy! Now!"

Andreas held her still. "It's not

that easy. We need to get you to a safe place. I promise you that I'll get him, okay? I'll go back for him."

She calmed and stilled, averting her eyes and looking out the window before looking at her husband again.

"Who are you?"

"I'm the same man who said 'I do' in church for you. I promised to love and cherish you, and I've never stopped."

She crossed her arms and stared out her window. After a moment, Andreas put the car back into drive and drove further away from Odhran's estate.

He was several miles away when she said, "Do you kill innocent people?"

"No, Phoebe. They're never innocent or even guilty of just one thing. Don't lose faith in me, babe."

She was quiet again. Andreas kept driving the car back to safety.

He knew that Harold didn't want the FBI to get involved, so he took her to Chung's. It would be better if the Bureau stayed in the dark about Harold's capture. The FBI's Hostage Rescue Team could get him out, of course, but at a very high cost. He needed a secure place to keep his wife, and there was a safe room in the back of Chung's. He had plenty of security, some of whom were more than capable of handling Odhran's thugs.

Phoebe was as safe as he could

make her now. She was just a pawn in Odhran's game, anyway — important to Andreas and Harold, but she was disposable to Odhran.

Harold, on the other hand, wouldn't be too healthy very shortly if Andreas couldn't quickly find a way to come through on his promise to his wife.

"What are you doing here, Andreas?"

"I need a safe room for my wife."

Chung looked at Phoebe. "It's a pleasure to meet you. How would you feel about eating some tiramisu?"

"That's my favorite!" Phoebe looked at Chung and then Andreas. "How did he know?"

Andreas winced. "Don't worry

about that. Just go with him."

"You're in luck. My sister is visiting at the moment. She can keep you company."

"Keep me company? What about my husband?"

"I'll be back later, honey. I made you a promise. I'm going to keep it. Time is of the essence."

"You promised." Phoebe bit her lip. "Come back with him, okay?"

"I'm going to do my damnedest." Andreas wished that he could kiss her for luck, but she was still mad about his deception.

Chung's sister came out of the restaurant and put an arm around Phoebe.

"Do you like Clueless? How about

we do a movie marathon?" Andreas knew that Phoebe would be in good hands at Chung's.

"We should talk. You barely gave me any details." Chung brought Andreas into his own office, the largest room in the back space.

"I just...I just exchanged my father-in-law for my wife."

"Okay. And?"

"I promised her that I'd get him back. I may need you to round up a few friends...unofficially."

"Let me know if it comes to that."

Delivery

Andreas

Andreas drove away from Chung's. He had the USB in his pocket, and he needed to go to Chip's.

He drove straight there. He had the USB in his hand, which he gave to the barista under the cover of a few bills.

"Hang on. You've got something waiting." The barista went into the backroom.

Were they giving him an assignment right now? It was the wrong time. His fists clenched.

Monsieur X had made it clear that he couldn't say no. He folded his arms over his chest while he waited. He leaned against the counter and tapped his foot.

Finally, the barista came out with a package in his hand and quickly poured black coffee into a cup. He accepted both things and brought it to a booth toward the back of the coffee shop. He pulled out the document.

It was a transcript of one of Harold's conversations from when he was researching the mega-weapon. The Crucible was a weapon with its own AI, a brain of its own.

It was clearly on the cutting edge of technology. Weapons that could detonate themselves were terrifying, frankly. It didn't rely on regular electricity, so it would never run out of energy as long as it could get a little light. It could hold solar charges for a very long time, and it could also find Wi-Fi networks under a cloak, so it could easily be accessed online.

It could do things that Andreas didn't want to think about. A weapon that could think for itself...that would have the capacity to bring around major civilian casualties that would change the entire political climate and influence Congress to write blank checks just like during Bush 43's administration.

Suddenly it made sense that Harold wouldn't give up the location of the Crucible. Giving it to a man like Odhran was basically handing over the country to an unscrupulous man.

There was a small note scribbled at the bottom of the document.

Gift. Followed by a research symbol that the Agency used. They were helping him extract Harold.

Suddenly, it clicked into place. They weren't asking him to murder his father-in-law. They'd known that all of this would happen, and they were telling him what he could do. It wasn't his final mission.

His resolve was strengthened. He had to get Harold back before it was too late. He shuddered when he thought of everything that Odhran could do to him before he got there.

He also knew that the Crucible could never land in Odhran's immoral hands.

No matter what.

Tea

Phoebe

Phoebe drank a little bit of oolong tea. "This is really good. Thank you for making it."

"No bother at all. You poor thing. You've been through quite an ordeal. I'm here for you if you need anything."

Phoebe just drank more tea and wished that she had something stronger, but she had to think of the baby.

She was tormented by the thought of Andreas waiting for her. He'd rescued her, true, but she didn't know if she wanted to stay married to him. Their whole marriage had been a lie. She thought that she fell in love with a five-star chef; the whole time, he'd kept his essential self a secret from her. She didn't know what to do. She put a hand over her stomach.

She turned to Atana and blurted out, "How do you know if love is real if you learn that you don't actually know someone?" She couldn't keep it inside anymore, and Atana was the first sympathetic ear that she'd gotten since she was kidnapped.

Atana put her hand over Phoebe's. She smiled at her.

"The true face of love is beyond circumstance, title, or appearance, sweetie."

Phoebe sat and turned that statement over and over in her head until Andreas knocked on the door.

She got to her feet. She looked into his eyes. She saw that he was wary.

He crossed the room and they hugged awkwardly.

Atana got to her feet, "I'll leave the two of you alone." She drifted out of the room.

"I'm so sorry about all of this, Phoebe. I couldn't tell you..."

"Just bring my dad home, okay?" She took his hands and laced their fingers together.

She looked up at his face. She could tell that he really wanted to repair their marriage, but she didn't know if she could find that much forgiveness inside of herself.

He brought her hand to his lips and kissed the back of it. "I will."

She pulled her hands out of his. She wasn't ready to be close to him, not when she still felt like he was an enigma.

Beating

Harold

Harold's head whipped to the side when another punch came to his face. He knew that he'd have enormous bruises when this was over.

"You gonna pass out like a wuss again, huh?" The thug who was wearing brass knuckles grinned at Harold. He had a bunch of gold teeth.

Harold spat blood onto the thug's shoes, which earned him another blow.

"It might be my job to hit you, but damn am I enjoying it. I could do this for hours."

Harold had already been there for several hours, but it was worth it. His baby daughter was safe now. He was sure that Andreas would make sure that nobody would ever be able to abduct her again.

Harold had been trained in resisting interrogation techniques from the best at the FBI. This here was like a walk in the park.

Red-hot pain exploded in Harold's head as a fist landed on the side of his head.

Well, maybe a very painful walk in the park. They hadn't used any tools yet. Harold knew that one reason why he was able to keep his mouth shut was because they hadn't gotten to the advanced techniques yet. He prayed that Odhran didn't use them. It wasn't a secret that the federal government used some questionable techniques to extract information from sources. It was hard to be on the other side, for sure. He might spend the rest of his very short life in Odhran's hands.

Whatever Odhran did, Harold couldn't talk. Too many innocent people would die as a result. If his silence meant that he would die while tied to this chair, then so be it. He knew what he was signing up for when he became an FBI agent.

"Enjoying your stay with us?"

"Just fabulous. Wonderful hospitality." Harold spat out some more blood.

Odhran said something else, but the words bounced off of Harold's ears. His ears were ringing and his head was spinning.

Harold might as well focus on the fuzziness. They were going to hurt him as badly as he could stand before dying, and if he didn't tell them where the Crucible was, they might kill him.

At least his daughter wouldn't pay the price with her innocent blood. He had saved her from being violated or murdered by Odhran, and that meant a lot to him. It was worth the sacrifice.

He thought about Sally. If he died here, he would regret leaving without telling her what was happening. At the same time, if Andreas found a way to break him out, he'd retire from the Bureau and take Sally somewhere warm, maybe Florida. She had always enjoyed freshly squeezed orange juice. He was getting too old for this sort of thing. It hadn't happened often, but recovery was definitely a bitch.

He hoped that he had the chance to recover from this.

Distractions

Phoebe

"Check mate!" Phoebe laughed and threw her hands in the air. She grinned at Atana and sat back, folding her arms over her chest with supreme satisfaction. Atana was a worthy opponent, but Phoebe had trained in chess at her father's knee.

Phoebe appreciated the challenge, and honestly she definitely needed to occupy her mind with something besides her mysterious husband and her father's kidnapping. It was like a reverse Beauty and the Beast situation. Odhran had her, but he was much more interested in her father.

She wondered when the Bureau would notice that her father was gone. Maybe Monday when he didn't come in. Should she try to stall them by having her mother call in to say that he was sick?

Her mother...was not going to be happy about any of this. Given a choice between Harold and Phoebe, Sally could easily go either way. Phoebe knew that Sally loved her, but Sally had loved Harold for longer.

Her head and heart were still adjusting to this very strange reality. She tried not to think about what they were doing to her father. She got the impression that they weren't making him dance.

She winced. Atana definitely had the right idea with the chessboard. She liked Atana a lot. They'd been fast friends from the first minute that they met. Atana was curvy and cheerful, which happened to be exactly what Phoebe needed right now. She was quiet enough to listen and attentive enough to let Phoebe know that she was listening. Phoebe had given Atana the bare details about what was going on and she had been suitably sympathetic. Phoebe tried to keep the worst of it out of the story, though. She didn't know much about Atana, and she didn't want to freak her out. She got the impression that Chung's might be much more than a restaurant if her husband had some kind of secret job, but she didn't know if she actually wanted to know the details.

"Are you feeling better after our movie marathon, homemade double chocolate gelato, tiramisu, extra butter popcorn, and chess?"

"I am."

She was feeling as good as she could feel under the circumstances. Andreas had left her. She couldn't help but worry about him getting into trouble, but she probably shouldn't worry. He was a professional...whatever...and probably knew a lot more about the clandestine life than she did.

Her stomach turned and she

clapped a hand over her mouth. She
didn't know if it was morning
sickness or fear for Andreas and her
father, but that popcorn and all the
sweet stuff wanted to come back up.

"You okay?"

"Just fine." Phoebe took her hand
away from her mouth and breathed
in through her nose. "Do you have
Monopoly?"

"Yeah, we do."

"Monopoly games last for hours,
even if there are only two people."

"Well, I think that sounds like a
great idea."

"Let's do it."

Atana knelt by a trunk and
opened it up to bring out a Monopoly
set.

Phoebe chose the hat while Atana chose the shoe.

She watched as Atana counted out the money for both of them. If she pretended like everything was fine, maybe it would be.

Ezra

Andreas

"Ezra."

"Andreas."

They slapped each other on the back just like old pals, but friends didn't charge as much as Ezra did. He was the top of the top. He made Dimitri look like the kid that he was. Dimitri was brilliant, but Ezra was old.

Ezra had done an enormous heist years ago, when banks were just switching to the digital age. He said that SSL was total shit, whatever that meant. Ezra had more than enough money, but he did a few jobs once in a while...if he was interested enough.

"You want to hack into the FBI?"

"Yup. I got a card."

Andreas winced just a little when he saw Ezra's eyes light up. He recognized that he was basically taunting a cocaine addict with a hit. Ezra was a hacker who was mostly retired, but it was his core. Ezra loved the game.

Andreas would have to keep an eye on the card if he didn't want Ezra to accidentally swipe it. It wasn't that he didn't trust him, exactly, but the ID was Mr. Kaine's. If it ended up in the wrong hand, it could definitely cause him some unnecessary problems.

"I'll leave you to do your work."

Ezra ignored him and typed quickly into his computer. Andreas looked at the keys. They weren't in the standard QWERTY layout, either. What was it with hackers and weird keyboards? Did they build them themselves?

When Andreas went to the counter of Chip's, he saw a little blackboard near the register.

"You offer hazelnut, vanilla, caramel, and mocha syrups now?"

"Yup. Fifty cents extra for a flavor shot."

"How about two cups of coffee? One vanilla and the other caramel. That should be enough." Andreas handed over a Chip's gift card, which was basically Monopoly money. When he remembered to use it, the Agency covered his coffee. If he got caught up in the lie that Chip's was actually a coffee shop, then he'd actually pay, but the cost of coffee was negligible considering the kind of contracts he did.

The barista poured out two cups of coffee and pumped a flavor shot into each one. He put on cup covers and coffee collars.

"Here you are."

Andreas held both of them in his hands and brought them back to the table where Ezra was waiting.

"They have flavor shots now."

"I don't want Chip's coffee. I've had it before."

Andreas smiled. Anybody who'd been here and had even one sip would know better than to try it out again.

Andreas drank slowly from the two cups while he waited for Ezra to do his thing. The sugar masked some of the burnt bitterness that characterized Chip's coffee. Apparently, the Agency sourced fair trade coffee which was roasted and ground somewhere in Africa. He was glad that they cared enough to handle it, but the coffee was also extremely foul. He drank coffee black, which meant that he would always taste the coffee exactly as it was: bitter swill.

After he looked at his watch, he

realized that Harold had been in their hands for too long already.

He hoped that Harold would hold on. He would be there as fast as he could possibly get there. He had a promise to keep.

Ezra turned his computer around.

"We're in. You need to move now before the next system sweep catches us in TS files."

Andreas didn't know much about government acronyms. "TS?"

Ezra rolled his eyes. "Top secret. Don't you watch movies?"

Andreas shook his head. "Nope."

"Speed it up. You don't have much time. The window is pretty small here."

Andreas clicked and typed his way around the files concerning the engineering company, the bank in the Caymans, anything he could find about Odhran Garin, and everything else. He used his phone to take pictures of the computer screen. He knew that Ezra had opened up a remote connection to the computers at the FBI, so he couldn't take any files and save them. There wasn't time to learn how to do it without having the FBI knocking on their door, anyway. Finally, he'd gone through everything that he could think of.

"I'm done. You're good."

Andreas watched as Ezra turned the computer back and began to type at a rapid-fire pace. It seemed that Ezra had been waiting for a chance to hack the FBI's files for a while; he knew what he was doing in there. Ezra had pushed him to get a little more time, but Ezra also knew about the security measures that the FBI used, which meant that he'd done his own recon before getting this job.

Andreas drank the slightly improved version of Chip's coffee while he flipped through the photos on his phone, scanning documents as he waited for Ezra to finish up and give back the card.

Finally, Ezra clicked something and closed his computer.

"That's it. Right now is the next sweep. They'll catch any connections are open right now."

"Card, please."

Ezra pulled the security card out of the computer and handed it to Andreas. "Do you have any idea how much something like that would cost on the open market? Enough to set you up for life."

"Not worth it," Andreas said. "Thanks for coming by."

"Thanks for the chance, man. Nothing to get your blood pumping like getting a sneak peek behind closed doors. I could FOIA all this, but it includes detailed security checks..."

"And nobody wants those."

"Right."

He slapped Ezra's shoulder.

"Gotta go."

Codes

Andreas

Andreas tossed the slightly less foul coffee into the trashcans by the door. He needed to go back to Chung's. He got into his car and drove back, his mind racing. He needed a second opinion on what he'd found.

Finally, he was back at Chung's. He parked and went inside.

Chung was cutting flank steak into small cubes.

"Need your eyes," Andreas said.

"Oye, Federico," he called to one of his kitchen staff. He pointed at the meat and Federico picked up the knife and finished up the job.

Chung wiped his hands on a blue towel. "How can I help you?"

"I want you to look over what I found when I got into the database."

"Sounds good. Let's go to my office." Chung threw the towel over his shoulder. He was dressed in a chef's whites, which were a nice shade of grey. You could tell the difference between novices and professionals at a glance. Real chefs got a little dirty.

The two men walked into Chung's office.

"Now, what do you have?"

"I have some images from things that I found when I reached into the

Bureau's information."

"Illegal."

"Do I look like I give a fuck?" Andreas took in a deep breath. "Sorry, man. I'm just on edge."

"Let me take a look." Chung ignored Andreas' outburst like it hadn't happened at all. He took the phone from Andreas' hand and sat back in his chair and frowned as he flicked through all of the images.

Andreas fought the urge to squirm in his seat. Every moment that it took him to figure out how to get Mr. Kaine out of there was a moment when Mr. Kaine would be tortured or worse.

"There's a lot of redacted stuff."

"I'm aware, yeah. I looked

through it already."

"So, the FBI recovered this weapon and confiscated it, then they moved it around."

"It didn't just sit in an evidence warehouse. I think that they understood just how potentially damaging it could be in the hands of terrorists."

"There are some codes here."

Andreas had only scanned the documents. "Codes? What kind of codes?"

"The fibbies got access to Odhran's surveillance system a long time ago."

"Yeah? Do we know if they're still active?"

"They might be." Chung squinted

at the image. He zoomed in on the document. "Well, it looks like this document was updated by some agent just a month ago, so these codes should still be valid."

Andreas smiled for the first time since he'd left Chip's.

"Good to know. That's very helpful."

"The system in question has a remote access feature."

"If they're smart, they would have turned it off."

"Not all criminals are very smart."

"Some are." They shared a grin.

"Some aren't." Chung tapped around on his computer. "He didn't close it off."

"Seriously?"

"Yeah, I just got in." Chung swung the monitor sideways so that both he and Andreas could see it.

"Nobody's at home."

Chung went through all of the cameras, but there wasn't motion on any of them.

"I'll look through your documents again to see if there could be more surveillance codes, maybe another system."

Chung's face had a look of intense concentration as he looked through the documents on Andreas' phone. Andreas could read at a normal speed, but Chung's ability to scan information and process it very quickly put him to shame.

"There aren't any more."

Andreas felt his smile melt away.

"What am I going to tell my wife?"

"Don't tell her anything yet. We'll keep looking. There has to be a way that we can extract him."

Andreas didn't want to ask, but he had to say, "What if he's already dead?"

"That old man is as tough as nails. He wouldn't give up that easily. Odhran really wants that weapon; I don't think that he'd kill his only connection to it."

Andreas got to his feet. He didn't want to be cooped up in Chung's office anymore. "Your sister is still with Phoebe?"

"Yup."

"I'm going to head over and check

on her."

"I'm going to pull the images from your phone and put them on my computer so that I can take a closer look."

"Thanks, man."

Andreas gave a nod to Chung before walking out the door and finding Phoebe in the cozy room where he had left her. She was sitting in a lounge chair with a cup of steaming tea, wrapped up in a soft pink blanket while watching a movie.

She had a look on her face that said that she wasn't paying too much attention to what was going on.

He felt like a failure for not keeping his promise to her, though it wasn't from a lack of trying. He wanted to walk in and take her into his arms, but he didn't want to disturb the moment of peace that they had carved out for themselves.

Instead, he backed out of the room without talking to his wife and went back to Chung's office. Maybe Chung could see another way of making progress through a different location. Andreas would take anything at this point.

When he walked into Chung's office, Chung was still looking through the documents.

"Any luck?"

"Not yet."

Andreas whipped out his phone and went through the images another time. He was missing something.

Maybe there was something there that would help them get Harold Kaine back, safe and sound.

Odhran owned a number of companies which were fronts for his criminal empire under a number of names, but he needed to find the most probable spot to stash Harold Kaine. Andreas got the impression that they weren't holding him where they'd held Phoebe. Phoebe didn't require maximum security. He loved her, and she was a smart woman, but she wasn't trained to resist cages.

Harold Kaine was. They'd probably buried him so far underground that it would be nearly impossible to find and rescue him.

Calling Home

Phoebe

Phoebe wasn't paying attention to the movie, but she noticed when Atana got to her feet.

"I feel a little bit cramped. I'm going to go hang out in the kitchen. You okay here by yourself?"

"Yeah." Phoebe appreciated Atana's company. "I'm fine."

"Be back in a bit."

Phoebe nodded and then watched her leave.

Phoebe pulled her phone out of her pocket. She needed to find the courage to call her mother. She hadn't done it yet, not wanting to tell her what exactly had happened to her father.

But what if something really bad happened? Her mother would never forgive her for keeping her in the dark, even if they were powerless. Her heart pounded as she tapped on her mother's contact info. She wasn't totally sure what she was going to say. She held her breath while she waited for her mother to pick up the phone.

Ring.

Ring.

Ring.

Phoebe's shoulders relaxed when the machine picked up. She was much more relieved than she should be. She hung up. She knew better than to leave a message for her mother; she listened to them once a year, if that.

There had been some nights when Phoebe grew up when her father didn't come home at night, and Sally Kaine would cry herself to sleep on those nights. They both knew that her father took all the precautions he could, but he faced off with dangerous criminals all the time. There could easily be a day when he didn't come home for good.

That day could be today. Phoebe wasn't looking forward to telling her mother that she had left her father to be beaten, tortured, and possibly killed. She didn't' imagine that the conversation would go particularly well.

Maybe Andreas would find him and save him. He said that he would. He also said not to lose faith in him.

Faith. Trust. Those were two things that were part of the foundation of any good marriage. He had broken hers when he'd hidden so much of himself away. She didn't even know what his job was, only that it involved guns and fake passports.

She was warm enough to fall asleep. Her pregnancy was making her sleep what felt like a hundred hours a week.

Lips

Andreas

Andreas stepped into the room to check on Phoebe. She was curled up in a little ball in the lounge chair that she'd been sitting in when he checked on her before. He clenched his inner muscles to walk quietly into the room, not making a sound. He traced the beautiful curve of her lips, her lush inky lashes touching her cheeks. The center of his chest ached while he watched her. She was his wife and the center of his universe.

She had pushed him away as if he were some kind of stranger. She was loyal, he knew that, but he had deceived her for a long time. She never would have married him if she had known the truth, and she would've run away like she did when she found his box of passports, money, and everything else that went along with his career.

He hadn't wanted her to find out that way. He had planned on telling her...maybe at some point in the distant future, when it was necessary, maybe after Mr. Kaine accepted him into the family.

It was one of the hazards of his job. He couldn't exactly meet her in that little coffee shop and tell her, "Hey, I'm a mercenary!" That's not how it worked. Everything was on a need-to-know basis, and Phoebe hadn't needed to know.

Until she did, and she left, because she'd found everything on her own. He was a fool for not covering his tracks better. It was convenient but stupid to keep his safe room in his own home. He should've rented a nondescript room or apartment somewhere else. He honestly didn't know what he would do if he lost Phoebe permanently. When she'd been kidnapped, he felt as if his heart were ripped from his chest and there'd been a big gaping hole left right in his center.

But when he had saved her, she'd fought him and hated him. And now she was staying here in Chung's, where she was safe.

Where would she go when the worst of the danger passed? She couldn't stay here forever. She could stay here for a long time, it was true. They had showers and everything. But eventually she'd want to leave.

Would she leave him for a second time? Harold Kaine was more than capable of keeping her safe from now on. Andreas knew that he didn't need to worry about that much.

He needed her. He'd never admitted it to himself, but she was the core of his being. She kept him on an even keel. Without her in his life, he knew that he was a stone-cold killer and not much more. He had planned for the short and medium term, but he hadn't had a long-term future before he met the beautiful woman who had changed his entire life.

It was funny that it wasn't his life that endangered hers; it had been her father's work that had inspired Phoebe's kidnapping. Nonetheless, Andreas knew that Harold Kaine was counting on him to keep his daughter safe, and Andreas would do the best he could to first get Mr. Kaine out of Odhran's hands and later keep Phoebe safe.

He pulled the blanket a little upwards to cover Phoebe a little better. She shifted in her sleep. Andreas had to turn away before he did something stupid and stole a kiss from his wife. He missed her.

Checking his watch, he walked out of the room. Chung might have more information now.

He walked into Chung's office.

"Anything?"

Chung just shook his head. Andreas gritted his teeth.

"Gonna go to the gym."

"I'll hit you if anything comes up."

Andreas went to the gym to hit the punching bags. He had a clock ticking in the back of his mind for all of this. He was out of resources. He had tried everything that he had. Now he was fighting to keep his hope alive, but it was a losing battle. He wondered what the conversation with

Phoebe would be like if Odhran killed Mr. Kaine. She would definitely leave him then. Andreas had always been at the top of his field with the Agency. He could always find a way, even if the hit was on someone who had seemingly impenetrable defenses. He took to his training like a duck to water when he'd first started, getting good marksmanship scores the first time that he tried shooting.

Why was he messing up now?

Emotions.

He'd never had a case before that directly involved the love of his life. He had never had his cover blown. He had never had all of his fake identities discovered before.

But he wasn't fake. He punched,

relishing the thud and the swing of the bag, which nearly hit the ceiling.

He had been a mercenary before he ever met her, but he regretted making that decision. There was no way that he could turn back from the life that he'd chosen; it was an irreversible choice because of the contractual clauses.

Shit.

He didn't want Phoebe to hate him. She meant too much for him to just walk away now that she knew the truth. He had to make her understand why he'd done what he did. He never meant to make a fool of her; it was the exact opposite of his intentions. He wanted to put together a foundation for them to have a little family, the kind of family he'd never had as an orphan.

He had another job after this one, but after that...he could leave this life behind.

If she would just stay married to him.

Crying

Andreas

Andreas took a very quick shower and used some of the clothes that he stashed at Chung's. He went upstairs to check on his wife again.

His heart squeezed painfully when he saw that she was bundled up in the blanket and crying softly, too quietly to attract any attention.

"Go away," she sniffed. "I don't want anybody to see me cry."

His heart felt like she'd stabbed him with a knife. He wanted to protect her. He needed to assure her. He'd promised her that he would make sure that her father was safe, but he hadn't been able to do it yet.

He knew that she wasn't ready to dive straight back into their marriage as if nothing had happened, but he couldn't stop himself from walking over to her and kneeling next to her chair. He needed to be near her like a flower needed sunlight. His heart was thumping in his ears. Getting close to his wife was as risky as coming near a hungry tiger. Maybe more dangerous. There was just so much at stake. He knew that she probably felt betrayed.

When he came closer to her, he reached out for her hand. She snatched it away from him.

"I don't want to talk to you right

now. You said that you'd get him back. You promised. I guess that it's as valid as our phony marriage..."

Andreas cut her off by kissing her deeply. She bit his tongue.

"Baby, I promise that I'm trying, okay?"

She cried harder. "I'm so afraid that my daddy..."

Andreas pulled her into his arms, tucking her face into the juncture of his neck and shoulder. She put her arms around him and cried her heart out. She made his shoulder wet as she soaked his shirt with her tears. He pulled her upwards, making her yelp. Then he sat in her lounge chair and held her in his lap, keeping her close.

"I know it's been a shock."

She wiped her eyes. "You think? As soon as I found that my husband wasn't the man that I thought that he was, I got kidnapped. And then my dad took my place. And we don't know when he'll be back."

Andreas stroked her hair, because he didn't have anything to say. He was at a total loss for words.

"Baby, I don't have much to give you. There's not much more that I can do to fix this."

Phoebe planted her mouth on his. After a moment of initial shock — Phoebe was still crying — Andreas responded. His arms tightened around her. She was kissing him back feverishly. Her body was rocking on top of his. He matched her intensity, bucking her upwards. He knew that their problems weren't fixed, but they could escape for just a little while.

Andreas stood up with his wife in his arms, with their mouths still connected. There were small bedrooms at Chung's, and he was going to beeline for one. He didn't want Chung's sister to walk in on them. He moved mostly by muscle memory, since he couldn't see much of anything beyond the tears caught in Phoebe's long lashes.

He felt with his hand for a doorknob, and then they were inside of the room. It was totally dark inside. He lowered Phoebe gently onto the mattress. He took off his shirt and everything else before he crawled into the bed with her.

"You up for this, Phoebe?"

"Yeah."

Phoebe reached for him and held him close to her. He felt the beat of her heart.

His hands went down to the bottom of her shirt before he peeled it off of her. His hands made quick work of her pants, even in the dark.

"Baby, did he...touch you?"

"No," Phoebe whispered. "Nothing like that."

Andreas felt anger boil in his veins that he even had to ask his pregnant wife a question like that.

"And...the baby?"

"I think the baby is okay. I can't tell anything is wrong anyway. But I don't know if I would know...it's my first pregnancy."

Andreas lowered his head and pressed his ear to her stomach.

"I don't know how to tell if anything's wrong either. Do you think that we should see a doctor?"

"Is it safe?"

"Maybe not." Andreas sighed. "If things were normal, we'd see one right away."

"But they aren't normal."

Andreas replaced his ear with his hand on her soft stomach. "I wish that things were different."

Lovers

Andreas

"I wish that you'd just told me beforehand."

"Would you have married me if you knew who I was?"

"Who are you?" she whispered.

"A man who loves you. Your husband. I promise that I never...I never meant to hurt you. I just had this job and one more until I was done. I was going to quit, I swear, especially with a baby on the way. I was going to do some catering for real."

"You are pure magic in the

kitchen."

"Just the kitchen, huh?" His hand went between her legs to touch her.

"Maybe other places, too," she admitted. He could hear the smile in her voice.

"Maybe?" Andreas lowered himself so that he could access the space between her thighs. He gave one long lick from top to bottom, savoring her sweet cream.

"Definitely," she whimpered, her hips bucking under him. He used his thumbs to pull her apart just a little further so he could get a little deeper. He would make her remember their connection, their marriage. She wouldn't leave him.

He used his hands to stimulate her clit while his tongue pushed inside of her soft opening.

"Oh," she said, her hips jerking.

He kept rubbing her clit until she was panting hard on the bed. She arched her back. He felt her muscles clench once, twice, three times, too many times to count. He pulled away from her as she shook with the aftershocks of her orgasm. He rolled to the side and then lay on his back and pulled his small wife on top of him, her thighs on either side of him.

"Ride me, Phoebe." He needed to know that she wanted him, too.

She steadied herself with two hands on his shoulders. Her mouth dipped down to meet his.

"With pleasure."

One hand went between them to guide his erection into her softness. They both moaned as he entered her.

"That's right, baby," he whispered. He didn't want Chung and the others to hear them having sex.

She slowly tortured him by lowering herself down centimeter by centimeter. He thought that he would go crazy before she took all of him.

Finally, she was fully seated on him. Her eyes were closed and her head was tilted back. Her mouth was hanging open.

"So full," she whispered.

His hands went to her curvy hips and held her in place as he bucked upwards.

"Ah!" she said.

"We have to be quiet, baby. I don't want anybody to come in here."

"I'll try." Andreas knew that Phoebe was normally pretty loud. He'd deal with it.

He sat up. Her arms went around his neck, then her hands were entangled in his hair and she was kissing him like her life depended on it. He rocked her gently on top of him, keeping up a steady rhythm until Phoebe was gasping against his mouth, fighting for breath. He broke the kiss and bit her neck.

She cried out as she went over, and he muffled her screams by kissing her again, holding her small body close to his as he found ecstasy.

Then the two of them slowly drifted back to earth.

"It's never...it's never been like that."

"We've always....but no, it's never been like that."

"I love you, Andreas."

"I love you, too, baby." He stroked her hair. "We'll find a way through all of this. I swear." He just hoped that he'd be able to keep that promise.

"I'm sleepy."

"Okay, honey." He withdrew from her body but instantly felt cold. He needed to clean her up, but she curled into the fetal position. Her breathing changed as she nearly instantly fell asleep. He pulled the covers up around her. She was naked, but he'd just make sure that he was the only one to go into this bedroom.

Andreas wasn't tired after they made love. He felt like a man with a new lease on life. She wouldn't leave him, or at least he thought that there was a high probability that she'd stay with him. He'd made a promise. Two. And now he had to find a way to deliver on them.

He could feel in his heart that Harold was still alive, which meant that he could still rescue him. He just needed to find out where he was being held.

Phoebe sighed quietly before going quiet again. He placed a kiss on her soft cheek. There was a time when he didn't have to ask for her faith in him. He knew that she'd trusted him totally.

And what had he done with that trust? He'd abused it by not telling her what he was. Who he was.

He turned on the light so that he could get dressed, even though he was still sticky. He needed to hit the shower and then bring something back to clean up his wife.

Andreas ducked into the showers, took a 30-second shower, and then found some paper towels which he moistened so that he could get most of it off of Phoebe. He went back into the bedroom and cleaned her up as much as he could. She'd have to do the rest when she woke up. He flicked off the lights in the bedroom. She should get some rest while she could. They didn't know what tomorrow would bring.

As he left the bedroom, Chung ran into him.

Boat

Andreas

"You found something?"

"Come into my office."

Andreas practically sprinted into his office. There was an open Heineken next to Chung's computer.

"What have you been up to?"

"I ran national property searches under some of the assumed names that the FBI has in its files about Odhran and his associates."

Andreas could see cars on Chung's screen. "You ran some traffic cams?"

"Nothing came up for any

vehicles registered to any of Odhran's aliases or any of his associates' aliases. I tried to run facial recognition on Harold, but we can't be totally sure that..."

"That Harold's face hasn't been mutilated beyond recognition." Andreas felt his jaw tighten. Damn. He needed more time with his punching bags. "I need a beer."

"Heineken okay?"

"Yeah."

He sat beside Chung as Chung took a beer out of a small fridge within easy reaching distance of his desk.

"You can't see them on any traffic cams. Why wouldn't Odhran stay at his house? It has to be the ideal place to extract information out of Harold. Why would he move?"

"You think that there's something secret at the estate?"

"Maybe. I know that Harold is alive. I can feel it. I know that I'm not deluding myself with a pretty fantasy. Where else would they take him and why? It wouldn't make sense to try to make it through customs with Harold. It's not as if Odhran is overly concerned with American law enforcement, not if he's kidnapped an FBI agent and is holding him for information."

"You think that he would be scared of you? You're a pretty big guy."

Andreas shook his head. "I don't

think that he considered me a threat. He might now know who I am."

"You want to go to the FBI?"

"No, not unless I want to end up in jail." Andreas snorted. "Wait a minute...what if he's waiting for someone?"

Andreas felt as if a lightbulb just went on in his head. He drank more of his beer. In vino veritas. He looked around the room. He looked at a boat in a glass bottle.

"That's a pretty boat," he told Chung.

"My parents had a boat like that once."

"Okay." He didn't know much about Chung, but he didn't want to be too nosy. Being too inquisitive didn't pay in their line of business.

He put his beer down. "Wait. There was a failed raid that took place in Chesapeake Bay, but the feds thought that it was dumb, bad intel. What if it wasn't bad intel. If Odhran had storage containers in Chesapeake Bay..."

"Then they could keep Harold Kaine there without anybody noticing. They are big enough to live in. Some people have turned shipping containers into homes. Zappos turned containers into Container Park in Las Vegas. It's a real possibility."

"Would anybody ever look for Harold Kaine in a shipping container?"

"Probably not. We've got the location from those documents, right?"

"Yeah."

"I'm going to get some reinforcements."

"I'll go check in on Phoebe."

Andreas went into the bedroom and looked at Phoebe, who was still curled up on the bed. She didn't stir an inch, but he knew that she was aware of him watching her and being inside of the room. He didn't want to wake her. He wanted to surprise her when he brought her father back. She had way too much stress lately, more stress than was really good for the baby. He stepped outside and gently closed the door.

He hung around the back side of Chung's. He needed to wait for back-up before he took on Odhran on his own turf.

Andreas had kicked his smoking habit a long time ago, but he went to the cabinet where he knew Chung kept his cigars and smoking supplies. He needed a hit right now.

Going into a secluded corner, he lit one cigar with a cheap Bic lighter. When he took his first drag, he choked. He was out of practice. He hoped that he wouldn't throw up like he did his first time as a kid.

He blew a smoke ring. The nicotine helped him loosen up just a little bit. He could make it there in time to save Harold. He could do it.

He told himself those things as if it would make it true. He could make it in time and bring Harold home safe to Phoebe and Sally. Odhran might not be breathing when everything was said and done, but then, he'd started it when he kidnapped Phoebe.

Stowaway

Phoebe

Phoebe woke up in the darkness and panicked a little bit, heart racing, thinking that she was still in her lavish prison on Odhran's estate. She relaxed a little when she remembered that she was at Chung's now.

She didn't know why, but she had a feeling that Andreas had a real lead. She turned on the lights and got dressed. She wasn't really all that clean, but she'd just have to deal with it.

Out the back door of the restaurant which led straight to a

parking lot, there were a few cars there. Andreas' SUV was out there.

She could hear them talking quietly. The wind carried their words over to her.

"Harold...bay...rescue..."

They really were going to get her daddy. Andreas would want to take his car; she knew that he liked to be at the wheel. She knew the code to get into his car too. Unnoticed by the men who had gathered for the rescue mission, she climbed through the car until she got into the backseat and hid under it, making herself invisible.

She waited for them to come into the car, but they took too long. She fell asleep.

* * *

When she woke up, she heard packs being loaded into the trunk next to her. Two guys were riding with Andreas, who, true to form, was driving his own car. The others must be in another car.

Finally, Andreas put the car into reverse and headed towards the Beltway.

Her heart began to beat as fast as a hummingbird's in her chest. Maybe she was crazy to stow away on this rescue mission. She didn't know what Atana would do if she realized that Phoebe wasn't at Chung's.

Maybe she was doing it because she didn't have complete trust in Andreas anymore.

Whatever it was, she felt as if she

needed to be on the real rescue mission. Maybe she'd be needed in some way and an angel whispered in her ear to nudge her into sneaking out. She might be very ill-prepared, lacking any kind of weapons training, and pregnant, but Odhran had her father. And Harold Kaine would come home safe tonight.

No matter what.

Phoebe felt the car go over what felt like every pothole in the DC metro. Seriously, did this SUV have no suspension at all? She knew that she felt more than usual since she was flat against the floor, but a particularly huge bump made her hit her head on the metal underside of the backseat.

"Ouch!"

She winced, not from pain. She knew that she'd been discovered when the car swerved over to the side of the road.

"Phoebe?" Andreas opened his door and opened the trunk. "Baby, are you here?"

She bit her lip and debated answering. It wasn't as if he hadn't heard her. There were two other people in the car.

"It's me," she admitted, crawling out from under the back seat and standing up. "Hi, Andreas."

"Are you serious?"

She blushed.

"Why would you do this?"

She blushed harder. "I don't even

know why I'm here."

"Let me introduce you to Ricky and Bill."

"Hi," she said, giving a small wave.

"Ricky and Bill and I...we go way back."

"Okay." She got the subtext. They were the same...the same kind of men as her husband.

Phoebe looked at Andreas and she could see irritation written plainly on his face. She had snuck into the car on impulse. She had no clue why she was here.

"Baby, you might see some stuff that you might not be ready for."

"I know," she whispered.

Andreas sighed. "It's too late for

us to take you back. Just stay hidden in the car, okay?"

"I will."

Phoebe was beginning to seriously regret coming on this ride. She didn't know why she'd inserted herself on this mission. But she was scared — scared that she might never see her daddy again.

They got back on the road and Phoebe had to admit that actually sitting on the back seat was much more comfortable than sitting on the ground.

She saw the men get out of the car. There was a truck next to them.

"My wife's in the back of my ride. It's a long story." Andreas closed his door, which muffled their voices so she could no longer hear what they were saying.

She swallowed hard. She told herself that she was okay sitting on the sidelines, but she could see all the men doing a double check of their weapons.

Andreas came around to the back of the car to take out the packs that they'd stowed there.

"You just stay in the truck, you hear?"

"I will," she said. She knew that it was silly to ride along with them, but she wasn't a child. She could follow simple directions.

"I'm sorry that I came."

Andreas nodded. "I'm going to put you in the truck, okay? Once you are there, don't move." His eyes were a dark grey and very serious.

"I won't."

He squeezed her shoulder and closed the trunk. Phoebe went out the side door of the SUV. Andreas helped her into the flatbed of the truck.

She was determined to stay out of sight while the mission to extract her father went on. She felt the truck roar to life and resigned herself to even more bumping, and not the fun kind.

Planning

Andreas

"Where'd you put her?"

"I put her in the truck. Nix stayed back to keep an eye on the cars and my wife. He's not built for this, anyway."

"Nah. He hasn't killed anyone."

Andreas tried to put his worry about his wife in the back of his mind. She should've been safe at Chung's. Now she was right next to the most dangerous person that she'd meet, one who had already kidnapped her once. He hoped that she'd stay put. She really shouldn't have snuck out. He couldn't imagine what his wife was thinking when she snuck into his car. It was ridiculously dangerous. She left a place of perfect safety to ride along in his car when he was wearing body armor. She didn't even seem to know why she was there.

Andreas took deep breaths as he ran through the hand signals that they'd use and their game plan for the extraction. Andreas knew that the men were prepared just as well as they could be. He undid the safety of his gun as he came near the warehouse that the Feds had raided before. Odhran was around here somewhere.

Andreas hoped that Harold Kaine

was conscious when they found him. He could only hope that the part of the interrogation where they began slicing hadn't happened yet.

He winced. He wasn't sure how he was going to explain any of this to Mrs. Kaine, who definitely had noticed at this point that her husband wasn't home.

"Showtime," Ricky said.

He needed to focus.

Damn it.

"Odhran," he shouted. "You didn't invite us to the party." He nodded at Bill, who began banging the butt of his gun on a big piece of metal that rang like a gong, making an incredible sound that spread throughout the whole dockyard. Bill immediately disappeared just like a ghost.

"What are you doing here, Andreas?"

Andreas spun around to look at Odhran, who was flanked by two men who looked like bodyguards. He was wearing a gold suit, making him look unreasonably flashy. For heaven's sake, they were in a dockyard. Who even wore suits here?

"Let's get on with it."

"Get on with what?" Odhran said, his tone light and innocent. He stepped into the dim lights of the warehouse. It was hard to tell where Odhran had come from, but that's why Andreas had brought a crew.

"It's a private party," Odhran

said, his tone icy. "But you're a big boy, aren't you? You know that already."

Andreas ground his teeth. Odhran acted as if Andreas hadn't killed more men than he could count on his fingers and toes.

He saw one of his crew members pointing to one of the containers. They knew which container Harold Kaine was in.

Odhran saw Andreas looking at the container. He raised his hand.

Immediately, Andreas felt a huge amount of force hit the center of his chest. He fell backwards. That bastard had his goons shoot him. He felt like he'd been kicked by a horse wearing an iron horseshoe.

He fell on his back and stared at the sky. To add insult to injury, he felt another shot go into his thigh. They must've realized that he hadn't bled when they shot him in the center of his mass. Andreas winced as he got to his feet and limped into the darkness, doing his best to weave through the narrow alleys of the containers. He needed to get closer to the one that Hawk had shown him had Harold Kaine.

Orange container. He needed to get closer to the orange container. He had to holster his gun because he had to try to staunch his blood-flow while he was on his feet and still walking around. If he had time, he'd tie a tourniquet there, but he didn't have that luxury.

He kept walking until he saw a glimpse of orange.

A bullet hit the container two inches from his face. He spun and shot in the direction the bullet had come from. The sound of a thud told him that he'd hit whatever thug was gunning for him.

"Andreas, right?" Odhran called out.

Andreas could hear the click of Odhran's fancy shoes. He really wasn't dressed properly for the docks. Andreas didn't answer Odhran's call.

He finally got to the orange container. He shot the lock off of it because he didn't have time to pick it. Inside, there was a guard who wasn't very alert. He pistol-whipped the man and shot him in his shooting arm before hitting him again to knock him out. He had an extra gun in his ankle holster. He put it in Harold's hands. His face was covered in blood and his eyes were swollen shut.

"Sorry it took so long, Harold. I had a little trouble finding you."

Harold didn't say a thing.

Andreas realized that Harold wasn't conscious; he was being held up by the duct tape that kept him attached to the chair.

He shook Harold's shoulder. "We're breaking you out, okay? Stay with me. Hold this gun. I'm going to unlock your handcuffs."

He rummaged around in the

unconscious guard's pocket until he found a key for the handcuffs. He undid the blindfold over Harold's eyes. Harold's pupils were different sizes. Definitely concussed.

Fuck. This was not ideal.

"Stay with me, Harold." He put a hand on Harold's arm to pull him out of the container.

Stepping out of the container, he immediately saw Phoebe held by one of the thugs dressed in black.

Fuck.

Triggers

Andreas

His heart was pounding hard when Andreas demanded, "Let her go." He raised his gun.

Odhran grinned at him.

"How about you make it worth my while, huh?"

"I know what you want. Let her go. I'll tell you what I know. If you hurt her..."

"We'll torture you until you tell us what we want to know anyway."

"I'll die before telling you a word about it. Harold might be trained in advanced interrogation techniques, but I was raised in foster homes."

Odhran raised a single brow. He motioned towards the container with his head. One of his thugs went inside to check the container, and he emerged a minute later with a nod and stood outside of the door.

Odhran stroked his chin.

"Let her go."

The thug holding Phoebe let her go. She ran straight for Andreas. He couldn't hold her, not now, but he felt a lot better with her by his side. They weren't out of the woods yet.

"You're bleeding. You have blood all over your pants." He could see the quick rise and fall of her chest. She was very close to hyperventilating and falling to pieces in the middle of a very tense situation. He needed to get her out of here and out of the line of fire.

"Baby, don't think about it. Can you go for a walk? Wait near where we parked the first time."

She raised her eyebrows.

"Please have faith. Everything will be fine. This is about business." He knew that Odhran was watching their exchange.

"Okay."

They watched as Phoebe walked away. Andreas kept half an eye on Odhran, ready to shoot if Odhran gave the order to murder her just for the fun of it.

Crew

Phoebe

Phoebe headed towards where they had initially parked when she was pulled behind a storage container with a hand over her mouth. She tried to wiggle away, but she couldn't.

"It's Bill. You should've stayed in the truck." Phoebe relaxed immediately. "Please get into this container. This is where the guys are staying right now. You should've let us get your father to safety." He finally let go of her mouth.

"I heard a shot and panicked; I

felt like I should run."

"You need to trust us, okay? We know what we're doing."

She bristled because he implied that she didn't know what she was doing. Drawing in a deep breath and trying to center herself, she went into the container with all the guys. Her heart thumped when she heard the door close, cutting her off from her husband.

She was breaking out in a cold sweat. She put a hand over her stomach and thought about what it would mean if her husband died tonight. Oh, her mother would make sure that she was taken care of, for sure. Her mom was very family-oriented.

But she didn't want her child growing up without a father.

In that moment, Phoebe made the decision to try to work it out with her husband if they both made it out of the docks alive.

She thought about what it would feel like if her husband died right here, right now.

Her heart ached. She knew that he was an essential part of her. Yes, he'd lied, and she'd make him make up for it. But she knew that she loved him and he loved her. The rest was window dressing. They'd work through all of it if they just tried.

Phoebe curled into a little ball and wrapped her arms around her knees, resting one cheek on her kneecap. Making that decision helped with a small measure of peace, but she still felt conflicted about her marriage. Andreas still had a lot of explaining to do for making a fool of her for that long. She wanted to hear his whole story before she forgave him completely.

Even though she was surrounded by an entire crew, she'd never felt so alone in her whole life.

All I Know

Andreas

"Where is the Crucible?" Straight to business. Odhran was tapping his foot, tension clear on his face. He'd kidnapped first Phoebe then Harold in order to find out where the weapon was, so Andreas knew that he wanted it more than anything. Nobody tangled with the FBI if they had any other alternatives.

"The FBI destroyed it." Yeah, it was a lie, but they weren't going to get their hands on the thing. Odhran would need to accept it eventually.

"Bullshit." Andreas blinked at

Odhran, who looked like he never cursed. He looked extremely proper, despite the overly shiny quality of his suit.

"It's gone."

"I know for a fact that it's not gone." Odhran pulled out a small .22-caliber gun. He took off the safety and pointed the business end at Andreas.

"Don't toy with me, boy. I want to know where it is."

Andreas grinned and said, "I only promised to tell you what I knew. That's what I knew. Scout's honor." Andreas held up his other hand, the gun-free one, in a mockery of the Boy Scout's three-finger salute.

Unimpressed with Andreas,

Odhran squeezed the trigger of his gun.

A shot rang out from behind Andreas. Odhran fell before he completed pulling the trigger. His thugs pulled out their weapons and exchanged fire with the rest of Andreas' crew as Andreas crawled low to the ground to get out of the crossfire. He saw that Harold was near him,b ut Harold was not in any shape to get into a gunfight.

"Sorry, Andreas." Harold headed towards the container.

"What the hell? Where are you going?"

Harold took the safety off of his gun. "Got something to do." He shot his guard in the head.

Andreas swallowed hard. It was stone cold to kill an unconscious man, but he probably deserved it if Harold Kaine was delivering death. He'd chosen the wrong man to follow. They stayed on the floor of the container until they couldn't hear any new shots.

They slowly walked up when all the thugs were down. Some of the crew stayed behind for cleanup — that's what the truck was for. The other guys got into Andreas' SUV. Harold took over the operation as he got into the car.

"We're going into an FBI medical center."

"Is that a good idea? You realize what we are, right?"

"Doesn't matter. I'll call you my CIs and tell them that you helped me catch Odhran. Close enough to the truth for my report about this whole ordeal."

"They know that you disappeared."

"Yeah."

Phoebe was sitting in the passenger seat, and Andreas knew that it wasn't all that safe to hold her hand while he was driving, but he didn't give a damn.

"Where are we going?"

"Someplace safe."

"Where?"

"I can't really disclose the address. Just follow my lead."

Andreas sat and thought about

it. He turned back to look at the men in his car. Some of them looked pretty rough; a few had bullet wounds.

"Let's go."

Harold Kaine gave them turn by turn instructions until they were in front of a nondescript business building in Herndon.

Medical Center

Andreas

"Herndon? Really?"

"Don't knock it."

Harold got out of the car. Andreas could see from the way that he was walking that nothing was broken, but he'd definitely been worked over.

"Just get inside before anybody can notice us."

Andreas and the rest of the crew got inside of the building.

As soon as the doors opened, Andreas understood why Harold had taken them there. It smelled like a hospital.

"Harold Kaine," Harold told the receptionist. "I need clean up."

"Right away, sir." The receptionist tapped his name into her computer and checked the photo that came up on her screen. "I'll have a team come downstairs."

Andreas was suddenly conscious of the enormous amount of blood soaking his slacks. He immediately walked over to a chair and nonchalantly sat down. The adrenaline had masked the fact that it hurt to walk.

"Andreas? Are you okay?" his wife asked.

"I got shot in the leg, babe."

"I know. And there's a hole in the

front of your shirt."

Andreas looked down. There was a hole from when they shot him the first time.

"It's okay. I'm wearing Kevlar." Or something slightly better.

There was a nurse with grey hair who came down to look at the whole crew. Most of them were unscathed, but Harold was in pretty bad shape, and Andreas knew that he had lost a lot of blood.

"Harold is going first, then you, then you." She pointed at Andreas and Phoebe.

"Me? I wasn't shot."

"You're pregnant."

"How can you tell?"

"The way that your hand is on

your stomach. No arguing." She pulled Harold towards an examination room. Andreas could see him wincing as he walked with bruises surely to be on his arms soon.

Andreas waited until he was checked out. They helped stop the flow of blood and quickly extracted the bullet before disinfecting the wound.

"You're going to need a wheelchair for a few days."

"Fuck that."

"Language!" Phoebe said. "What about the baby?"

"I don't think that the baby can hear me in utero, babe."

"Still."

"You're pregnant." The second nurse, the one who checked Andreas, looked at Phoebe. "Would you like a little ultrasound?"

"Please."

She went out the door and came back pulling a cart.

"The gel is a little cold, but I think that you can handle it."

She motioned for Phoebe to get on the bed. She climbed up next to Andreas. Andreas got off and limped to a chair.

"Shirt up, please."

The nurse smeared gel all over Phoebe's stomach before putting the ultrasound device on her. There was a monitor on the cart that Phoebe fixed her eyes on.

"Andreas! Do you see our baby?"

"Yes, I do." He had to clear his throat, which felt choked up.

Phoebe was crying happy tears. He limped to the bed to hug her.

"I'll just wipe off the gel and then leave you two alone. A doctor will be in shortly." The nurse grabbed paper towels from a dispenser, wiped down Phoebe's stomach, and left the room.

"We're going to be okay, babe. I know that I let you down, but..."

"You kept your word."

Andreas locked his eyes with her.

"You kept your word. My father is just fine. All of this would've turned out very differently if you weren't....you. Exactly you. I'll just have to relearn who you are. Your training saved us all."

Andreas could tell that she was still turning all of it over in her mind.

"You're my miracle, Phoebe. I love you with everything inside of me — everything that I have."

Smiling, she said, "I know. Me, too."

Andreas knew that they would be just fine.

"Let's start from the beginning. I'm Andreas. I grew up in the Nelson Hill Houses. I was made more than I was born..."

Epilogue I

"Pass the peas, please." Harold grinned at Andreas as he asked it. He had become a lot warmer after Andreas saved his life, but he still loved to give him a hard time.

Andreas handed him the peas, which were mixed with gooey cheese. They were the best peas that Andreas had ever had in his life.

"So, is there anything else that you'd like to get off your chest before you're properly initiated? Family? Friends?"

"Initiated?"

"Answer the question."

"Uh...no. I can't think of

anything."

"Splendid. You'll do the dishes tonight."

"Dishes?"

"You heard me, son, unless all those gunshots impacted your eardrums. Take you initiation like a man."

Harold winked at him before shoving the serving spoon under the peas and getting a big helping.

Epilogue II: First Birthday

"Ma? Ba? Da?"

"Yes, your daddy and mommy are right here for you, sweetness." Sally leaned in and kissed Zoey's little face, which was covered in green frosting.

HAPPY BIRTHDAY wasn't legible anymore, but Andreas was glad that they had the Kaines over for Zoey's small birthday party. Zoey was wearing a dark green dress that was also covered in frosting.

"What in the world?"

Andreas looked at Sally. Her hand was on Zoey's chubby little thigh.

"How did she get frosting on the

toes of her tights?"

All four of them looked at Zoey, who had smeared frosting on her face, hands, and dress. But none of them had noticed that the frosting was on her tights.

"I'll take care of it." Phoebe got to her feet and reached for Zoey.

"I'll help you clean her up." Sally got to her feet, too. The two women left the room with the baby carefully cradled in Phoebe's arms.

Andreas was on a first-name basis with Phoebe's parents after the whole ordeal. Phoebe had worried that the stress of the kidnapping and the subsequent rescue mission for Harold would hurt the baby, but Zoey had been born with an Apgar score of six, so she was totally healthy.

"I'm proud of you two."

Andreas raised his eyebrows at his father-in-law.

"Yeah?"

"I think that you're doing a good job with your daughter. I remember how nervous I was when Phoebe was born. You've been far more involved with your child than I was. That's one of the things that I regret the most, especially now that I've retired from the FBI. Family is the one thing that matters most, and it's easier to see in retrospect."

Andreas nodded. "That's why I retired." Andreas winked as Harold laughed.

"You're a little young to retire,

but how is your catering business doing?"

"Pretty well. We're associated with one of the biggest wedding venues in DC, so we're pretty busy."

"Good to hear. If you want to get a little one-on-one time with Phoebe, we'd be happy to have Zoey over to our house. Phoebe said that she started sleeping through the night."

Andreas felt his heart leap. Andreas loved Zoey to bits, but privacy and alone time with Phoebe had taken a toll. Zoey had colic for the first few months of her life. She woke up a few times each night, so both of her parents were bone-tired.

But she'd finally stopped crying, and Andreas had recently begun sleeping a whole seven hours, which was pure bliss.

"I'd be glad to take you up on that offer. I'll talk to Phoebe about it and she'll handle the details."

After Zoey's birth, Phoebe had left the dance troupe and gone full-time into her Etsy business, which had been featured in several magazines because she was one of the most successful female entrepreneurs in the DC region.

Sally came back down the stairs with a big wet mark on her shirt.

"We gave Zoey a quick bath, but she was...very enthusiastic about it."

Andreas grinned. "I gave up on trying to stay dry a long time ago. Zoey loves bath time."

Sally looked down at her shirt ruefully. "I need to change."

Harold got to his feet. "Well, it was wonderful to celebrate Zoey's first birthday with you, but I've got to get to the golf course in an hour. I'm meeting one of my old partners to informally consult on a case. Let's get you home, Sally."

Sally linked her arm with Harold's.

"Tell Phoebe that we said goodbye."

"Will do."

Andreas watched his parents-in-law walk out the front door. He heard the roar of the engine starting as they backed out of the driveway and went home.

Andreas went upstairs to go find Phoebe. She was walking in a slow circle around Zoey's bedroom. Noise didn't bother Zoey, but she did wake up every few hours. When Zoey refused to sleep through the night, her crib was kept in her parents' bedroom. But now that she was a good sleeper, she'd migrated into her own room. Phoebe insisted on keeping a baby monitor at full volume on the nightstand on her side of the bed, though.

She was humming softly to Zoey, whose eyes were drooping. Her little mouth opened in a perfect oval, flashing the teeth that were coming out. She'd been very fussy when they came out when she was six months old, but they'd bought ice teething rings, which had helped a lot. Phoebe had freaked out when Zoey ran a little fever, but they'd looked it up. It seemed that it was normal for babies to run a little fever while they were teething. Phoebe had still gone on an intense cleaning spree. Their house was practically kept at "clean room" standards. He considered himself lucky that Phoebe didn't make him dress in a HAZMAT outfit.

He leaned on the doorframe as Phoebe gently put their baby in her crib.

"All good?"

"Yup."

Phoebe turned on the baby monitor and went outside of the

baby's room, closing the door.

"Well, your parents are gone and our little one is knocked out."

Phoebe looked down at her shirt, which was drenched like Sally's had been.

"I need to clean up."

"You want me to help?"

Andreas saw a little spark in Phoebe's eyes.

"You want to take a shower together?"

"Yeah."

Phoebe walked straight into their bedroom and beelined for the bathroom, shedding her clothing on the ground on the way.

Andreas loved the way that her hips moved when she walked. In the bathroom light, her dark skin glowed with a soft shine.

"Have I told you how lucky I feel to be married to you?"

"Not lately."

"Let me show you."

Andreas took off his own clothes, which joined Phoebe's on the floor. He came into the bathroom and pinned Phoebe against the wall, keeping her in place with his hard body.

He bit her ear before biting his way down the center of her body, going past her neck, her breasts, her soft stomach which still had the signs of her pregnancy, and right down to her core.

He parted her thighs a little bit so

that he could lick the juncture of her thighs. She was wetter than a sauna.

His tongue penetrated her softly. He put his thumb on her clitoris, pushing and rubbing it. He could hear her gasping. Her hips jerked forward.

He stopped. He wanted them to come together.

"Let's get into the shower." He pulled her into the shower with him and turned on the water, which fell all around them.

He turned her so that she was facing the back of the shower.

"Hands on the shelf."

They had a shelf in their shower where they kept their shampoo, which was about two feet high.

Phoebe bent over and put her hands flat on the shelf. Andreas appreciated the view before his hand went to stroke the curve of Phoebe's luscious hip before circling to the front of her body to rub her again.

"Take me," she demanded.

With one hand, Andreas pressed the tip of his hardness between her legs.

Then he was pushing inside of her tight body. Even after the baby had come, Phoebe still felt like a dream.

Sometimes he thought that his life with her was a dream, one that he'd never even dared to have as a kid. He had a family now, and he'd do anything to keep them safe and happy.

He pushed all the way inside of his wife. Phoebe moaned in front of him, pushing her hips back to try to take him even deeper.

"How would you feel about another baby?"

"Well, I'm not on birth control, so..."

Andreas pumped inside of her, thinking about having another kid. Maybe another little princess like Zoey or a young rascal who would be a terrible troublemaker.

"I'd like to have a dozen kids."

Phoebe laughed, which did interesting things to the connection between their bodies.

"Whoa, there. Let's start with two

and go from there."

Andreas pumped inside of her again. She stopped talking as he began to pick up the pace.

Finally, he felt her inner muscles clench around him sporadically. He knew that she was climaxing because she was panting hard, gasping.

And then he was following her, shooting his seed inside of her body.

Andreas pulled himself out of her. They wordlessly reached for soap and cleaned each other up in the shower, stealing kisses while they washed each other.

When they were reasonably clean, Andreas turned off the water and grabbed a towel to dry off Phoebe. She took it from him and

THE HITMAN'S PREGNANT BRIDE

wrapped it around herself.

Andreas reached for his own towel and put his arm around his wife's shoulders as they walked out of the bathroom.

He leaned down to whisper in her ear, "I love you."

"I love you, too."

Deleted Scene: Prologue

Andreas

Andreas was walking down the street when he passed a coffee shop and did a double take.

There was a girl in the window, a girl who was drawing a jagged heart with her finger on the window pane. His eyes lit up for the first time in what felt like years. He couldn't remember the last time when someone had captured his attention like this. Sure, there were plenty of girls — girls everywhere — but none like this one. His heart was pounding a little faster than usual.

The girl in the coffee shop reminded him of some kind of modern-day Snow White because of her hair cut. She had dark hair which was sharply cut on an angle that just touched her shoulders. She had luscious lips that were spread in the most beautiful smile he had ever seen.

He ran his hands through his hair, trying to check that everything was lying flat. He didn't want to look like a dork when he met this lady for the first time. He took a deep breath before he went through the coffee shop door, making the bells jingle. He stood in line and ordered some kind of caramel macchiato drink before he pretended to survey the store. To his satisfaction, every seat was full.

"Hello," he said, walking over to the girl's table near the window.

"Hello," she said, her smile broadening as she looked at him.

"Every seat is taken. Would it be okay if I sat at your table?"

"No problem."

He could see the book that she was reading.

"Darkest Touch?"

Her cheeks flushed as she said, "Yes."

"You like paranormal romance?" He had never read any of Gena Showalter's books, but he knew that some people liked that kind of thing.

"I do."

"How about for our first date, I

take you into a bookstore and buy you any book that you want?"

She blinked for a few seconds. "You would do that?"

"Yes, absolutely."

"Do you want to have our first date right now?" She licked her lips and eyed his pecs. "I've lived for twenty-two years, but I've never had anyone offer that to me."

"Let's go."

She slipped her book into her tote bag, which said "Real Woman. Real Men. Real Romance." on it, and then she walked towards the door. Andreas had his cup of coffee in his hand, but he dumped it in the trash as he left. The coffee mattered very little; he had only purchased it to have an excuse to talk to her. He ran after her as she went into the tiny independent bookstore next door.

* * *

ONE YEAR LATER

Andreas was bemused to find himself in an apple orchard. Phoebe had asked for an apple-picking date. He had never done anything like this — not a big nature guy — but he was very surprised to find that he liked it. Phoebe kept asking him to pick her up so that she could reach apples on higher branches. He loved the excuse to touch her curvy body.

"Eek!" Phoebe said, big drops of water landing on her shoulders and leaving big marks where they landed.

Andreas shrugged off his coat and raised it over both of their heads, drawing Phoebe close to him.

"Let's run for it!"

Phoebe wasn't as fast as Andreas, but then, she didn't train for lethal speed. He was careful to run at her pace. She was laughing joyfully while they ran for the closest shelter, which was the edge of the roof of the main building.

When they got there, Phoebe turned to Andreas, slipping her arms around his neck and tugging him downwards.

"My hero," she said, the light of laughter still in her eyes.

Andreas leaned down to kiss her, putting his hands on the small of her back and pressing her small body against his larger one.

Phoebe broke the kiss. "We left the apples."

"We can get them when it stops raining."

"How should we pass the time?"

"I think I have an idea." He turned swiftly so that she was in his arms, then he pressed her body against the wall. He explored her mouth thoroughly as they waited for the rain to stop.

An eternity later, he told her, "I think the rain stopped a while ago." His voice was low.

"Why don't we go back to your place?" Phoebe's hand trailed low on his back.

After running for the apples that they had picked and the potatoes that they had bought when they arrived, Andreas held them in his arms. His hands were still free. Andreas pulled her towards the car and broke every speed limit on the way home.

* * *

ONE HOUR LATER

Phoebe came out of the shower with her hair wrapped up in a towel.

"Can you set the table?"

"Sure thing."

Andreas looked down at the skillets that he had on the stove. Those delicious apples that they'd just picked were frying in some butter and cinnamon, filling the kitchen with their scent. He had some potatoes from the same farm baking in the oven. He'd rolled them in salt and pierced them with forks; the nice thing about baked potatoes was that they tasted nicer the less that you did with them. He had another skillet with a bunch of mushrooms cooking in some beef stock to give them a savory flavor.

He knew enough about cooking to maintain his cover. As far as Phoebe knew, he was a highly skilled chef. Even without a restaurant of his own, or even a branded cookbook, he'd sold the lie. He could do interesting things to entrees, and Phoebe laughingly called him her food whisperer. He'd never tell her about the hours that he spent testing food to make the best version of her favorites.

He thought about the ring in a small box in his pocket. He was sweating, and it wasn't due to the heat of the kitchen.

He didn't really know much about proposing, since he'd never done it before. He knew that he was supposed to get down on one knee, but that was it.

The mushrooms looked like they were done. The apples were nice and brown, too. He turned off the heat and put the pans on cold burners.

Phoebe's arms wrapped around his waist.

ALYSE ZAFTIG

"Is that a rolling pin in your pocket, or are you happy to see me?"

Andreas' heart beat faster than it did when they had run earlier that day. Was this the right moment? He had no idea.

"It's not a rolling pin."

Her arms tightened. He could feel her press against his back.

"Yeah?" Her hands traveled downwards.

He caught them before they could go below his waist. He spun around and knelt in front of her.

"What are you doing? Did you drop something?"

Instead of answering, he reached under his apron and pulled out the blue box before opening it. The ring

374

caught the light from the kitchen's stainless steel overhead lamps.

"Is that?"

"Phoebe Kaine, would you do me the great honor of marrying me?"

Her hands went over her mouth. Phoebe was totally speechless. Her eyes were wide with shock.

"Yes!" She grabbed the box and slid the ring onto her finger. She pulled him up and kissed him, wrapping her whole body around his much bigger one.

"I can't wait to make you mine," he whispered in her ear. He bit it hard, hard enough to make Phoebe yelp.

"I can't either. I should do the whole shebang — my parents, my friends, my pastor — but I'd rather just run off to Vegas with you."

"You deserve the best wedding ever, but I don't want to wait. We can do a reception when we get home, okay? We can tell them then. But we'll just grab last-minute tickets and do the deed in Vegas right now."

"Let's go."

for mature audiences only. Names, characters, places, and incident either are the product of the author's imagination or are used fictitiously. Any resemblance to events, locales, business establishments, or actual persons, living or dead, events, or locales is purely coincidental.

All sexual activities depicted occur between consenting characters 18 years or older and who are not blood related.